THROUGH
FAIRY HALLS
OF
MY BOOK HOUSE

EDITED BY

OLIVE BEAUPRÉ MILLER

PUBLISHERS

THE BOOK HOUSE for CHILDREN

CHICAGO

PREFACE

"THROUGH FAIRY HALLS" is intended for boys and girls who have reached the age when, with ever expanding imagination, they are most interested in the fantastic adventures of wonder tales. And the boys in particular have a still stronger need for some stories with quick, dramatic, violent action, such as "Jack the Giant-Killer" and "Chylde Roland and the Goblin King."

So this volume abounds in adventurous folk tales from many different countries, like "The Princess on the Glass Hill" from the Norse; "The Good Comrades of the Flying Ship" from the Russian; "The Lost Spear" from South Africa and "The Strong Boy" from Canadian Indian folklore. It has humorous tales as well, such as "Daniel O'Rourke" from the Irish; "The Squire's Bride" from the Norse; "The Three Wishes" from the Spanish and "The Three Sillies" from the English. And it also includes a few of the more poetic tales like "The Sleeping Beauty" from the French and "The Moon-Maiden" from the Japanese.

The Bible is represented in this volume by the adventurous story of "Daniel in the Lion's Den." And here for the first time you will find one of Shakespeare's plays retold. Since boys and girls are now in the fairy tale age, the play selected is "A Midsummer Night's Dream," which centers on Oberon, Titania and all their following of elves and fairies. Naturally Shakespeare belongs in the literary background of every child, since he will meet references to Shakespeare all his life. In various volumes of My BOOK HOUSE we have four of Shakespeare's plays retold—"A Midsummer Night's Dream," "The Tempest," "The Winter's Tale," and "As You Like It" in addition to a number of rhymes and verses from Shakespeare.

Tied up with fairy tales in Volume Six, is "The Fairyland of Science," which tells the story of how Jean Henri Fabre, the great French naturalist, discovered in the lives of the little jeweled insects of his garden, the Fairyland of Science.

Here, too, the theme of art and music is carried on as it has been in all the books. In "The Wonderland of an Artist's Workshop" Leonardo da Vinci is presented, not only in his capacity as an artist, but with his studio full of noisy apprentice boys all eagerly interested in trying out the new flying machine Da Vinci had just invented. And in "The Boy Who Made His Own Materials," a boyhood incident from the life of Titian is given.

As to music, we have in this volume "A Musical Visit to Fairyland," which tells how Felix Mendelssohn wrote the music for "A Midsummer Night's Dream," and "The Duty That Was Not Paid," a story of Mozart in childhood.

Thus these stories in "Through Fairy Halls" relate music, art and science to literature in the period when boys and girls are of an age to wander freely in any sort of Wonderland.

CONTENTS

		PAGE
APRIL	John Galsworthy	97
ARUMAN, A HERO OF JAVA		202
ASSEMBLING OF THE FAYS, THE	Joseph Rodman Drake	25
BOY WHO MADE HIS OWN MATERIALS, THE	A Story of Titian	114
BOY'S SONG, A	James Hogg	96
CHYLDE ROLAND AND THE GOBLIN KING	An English Folk Tale	11
DANIEL IN THE LIONS' DEN	From the Bible (The Book of Daniel)	180
DANIEL O'ROURKE	Adapted from the Story by T. Crofton Croker	62
DUTY THAT WAS NOT PAID, THE (Wolfgang Mozart)	Katherine Dunlap Cather	159
FAIRY FORESTS	Alfred Noyes	190
FAIRYLAND OF SCIENCE, THE	A Story of Jean Henri Fabre	184
FISHERMAN WHO CAUGHT THE SUN, THE	A Hawaiian Legend	198
FOUNTAIN, THE	James Russell Lowell	224
GOOD COMRADES OF THE FLYING SHIP, THE	A Russian Tale	26
HIE AWAY, HIE AWAY	Sir Walter Scott	70
HOW YEHL, THE HERO, FREED THE BEAMING MAIDEN	An Alaskan Legend	102
"IT"	James Whitcomb Riley	131
JACK THE GIANT-KILLER	An English Folk Tale	140
JUDGING BY APPEARANCES	Emilie Poulsson	33
LITTLE NELL AND MRS. JARLEY'S WAX-WORK	Arranged from The Old Curiosity Shop by Charles Dickens	213
LITTLE PICTURES FROM FAR JAPAN		196
LITTLE SHEPHERD'S SONG	William Alexander Percy	173
LOST SPEAR, THE	A South African Tale	132
LUCK BOY OF TOY VALLEY, THE	Katherine Dunlap Cather	108
MAN WHO LOVED HAI QUAI, THE	An Indian Tale of Mt. Tacoma	127
MERMAN, THE	Alfred Tennyson	178

                                                                          PAGE
MICE, THE   .   .   .   .   .   .   A Winnebago Fable   131
MIDSUMMER NIGHT'S DREAM, A .   Told from the Play by William Shakespeare   36
MR. MOON   .   .   .   .   Bliss Carman   34
MOON-MAIDEN, THE   .   .   .   .   .   A Japanese Fairy Tale   210
MUSICAL VISIT TO FAIRYLAND, A   .   .   A Story of Felix Mendelssohn   58
OFF WE'LL GO .   .   .   .   Basho   196
PIGLING AND HER PROUD SISTER .   .   .   William Elliot Griffis   191
                       A Korean Cinderella Tale
PRINCESS ON THE GLASS HILL, THE   .   .   . Sir George Webbe Dasent   80
PROVIDENCE   .   .   .   .   Joseph Addison   79
SLEEPING BEAUTY, THE   19
SNOW   .   .   .   .   Ransetsu   196
SNOW BLOSSOMS   197
SONG FROM "THE FLOWER OF OLD JAPAN," A   .   .   Alfred Noyes   209
SQUIRE'S BRIDE, THE .   .   .   .   . Peter Christen Asbjörnsen   98
STRONG BOY, THE   .   .   .   .   .   . A Canadian Tale   118
THREE SILLIES, THE   .   .   .   .   .   . Joseph Jacobs   174
THREE WISHES, THE .   .   .   .   .   A Spanish Fairy Tale   92
TROPICAL MORNING AT SEA, A   .   .   .   Edward Rowland Sill   201
TWELVE MONTHS, THE   .   .   .   . A Czechoslovakian Fairy Tale   71
WILD FLOWERS   .   .   .   . Peter Newell   69
WILLOWS IN THE SNOW   .   .   .   .   .   .   Tsuru   197
WISE MEN OF GOTHAM, THE   170
WONDERLAND OF AN ARTIST'S WORKSHOP, THE   .   .   .   .
                                      A Story of Leonardo da Vinci   164

Chylde Roland and the Goblin King
An English Folk Tale

ONCE there was a youth, named Roland, who, being of noble birth, was called by the title of Chylde, as were all sons of the nobility. Now Chylde Roland had two brothers and a beautiful sister, Burd Ellen. One day all three brothers and their sister were playing ball on the fine green lawn between the castle and the churchyard. At last Chylde Roland, who was the youngest of the brothers, kicked the ball with his foot and caught it with his knee, then tossed it so high in the air that it flew up over the church tower. Laughing, Burd Ellen chased it. Around the church she ran.

Chatting gaily and fearing nothing, the brothers waited for their sister to bring back the ball. But she did not return. At last they grew anxious and looked for her all round the church. But she had vanished! They could not find her. So in great distress they sought her through all the land. And still she was nowhere, nowhere to be found.

Then the brothers and their mother grieved greatly. And since the maiden's father was dead, the eldest brother went to ask Merlin, the old wiseman and magician, if he knew where Burd Ellen was.

"Wherever she is I'll find her and bring her back!" the youth vowed.

"That's easier said than done!" the white bearded old wiseman said. "For, alas! the poor maid must have gone round the church 'widershins'—which is to say from west to east, contrary to the way the sun goes. If that be true she was carried off by the King of Elfland, the most malicious, the most to be dreaded of all the goblins who ever troubled the world. And she is now a prisoner in his Dark Tower. To bring her back from there would take the boldest knight in Christendom!"

"I'll save her or die in the attempt!" her brother cried.

So Merlin told him what he should do in that dark land of evil goblins and the eldest brother set out for Elfland.

Then his brothers and his mother waited for him to return. Long they waited and longer still. And every day their doubt, their sorrow, their fear lest he had met calamity deepened.

So the second son went to Merlin and asked the same questions as his brother had. Then he, too, set out to find Burd Ellen.

Again the mother and her youngest son, Chylde Roland, waited. Long and longer still they waited with growing doubt and sorrow. But this brother also failed to return. So Chylde Roland asked his mother, the Queen, to let him go. But at first she would not, for he

12

was the last of her children. However, he begged and begged, until at last she let him go. And she gave him his father's good sword that had never struck in vain. Then Chylde Roland said good-bye to his mother. Going to the cave of Merlin, he, too, asked the necessary questions.

"Well, son," said Merlin, "you have only two things to remember. But simple as they seem, they're very hard to do. First you must remember that everyone in Elfland, no matter how pleasant and kind he may appear, is a goblin, an evil enchanter. So if anyone speaks to you there, you must out with your sword and off with his head. The second thing which you must not forget is this—in Elfland you must eat no bite and drink no drop, no matter how hungry or thirsty you may be, for if you should either eat or drink you will never see Middle Earth again!"

Nothing daunted, Chylde Roland thanked Merlin and off he went on his way. Far, far, and afar, he journeyed. Then at last he saw a horse-herd tending some coal black horses. And the horses had fiery eyes that shot forth sparks and flame. So Chylde Roland knew that he was now in the dark realms of Elfland.

"Canst thou tell me," he asked the horse-herd, "where the King of Elfland's Dark Tower is?"

"I cannot tell thee!" The horse-herd smirked in an ugly attempt to look pleasant. "But go on a little farther and thou wilt come to the cow-herd. Mayhap he can tell thee!"

Then, without another word, Chylde Roland drew the good sword that had never struck in vain, and off went the horse-herd's head with the smirk still on his lips.

From there the youth went on till he came to the cow-herd, of whom he asked the same question.

"I cannot tell thee!" The cow-herd smirked also. "But go on to the hen-wife. She is sure to know!" Then Chylde Roland outs with his sword and off goes the cow-herd's head.

After that he went on to the ugly old hen-wife. In answer to his question she took him to the edge of the woods and said:

"Dear lad, from here thou canst see the Dark Tower on top of yonder green hill that rises up in terraced steps. If thou wouldst enter the tower, go round it 'widershins,' three times and each time say:

>" 'Open, door! Open, door!
>Let me come in!' "

Well, Chylde Roland had no mind to cut off an old woman's head but now he saw her eyes grow as fiery as those of the horses. Then he knew that she, too, was a goblin gladly sending him on to that frowning, threatening tower in the hope that he might never leave it alive. So he outs with his sword and offs with her head.

14

THROUGH FAIRY HALLS

Then he went on till he came to the tower. Three times he went round it "widershins," saying each time:

"Open, door! Open, door!
Let me come in!"

And, the third time the door did open, but when Chylde Roland went in, it closed with a click, and he found himself in the dark. By-and-by he saw that he was not in actual darkness but in a kind of twilight. For though the place had neither windows nor candles, its walls were made of transparent rock, incrusted with silver and bright stones. So he went down this passage till he came to two tall, wide folding-doors. And when he went through them he saw a most glorious sight. For he was now in a spacious hall, having pillars of gold and silver, entwined with wreaths of flowers which were made of diamonds, emeralds, and other precious stones.

From the center of the high, arched ceiling an immense lamp swung on a golden chain. It was made of one big pearl hollowed out and quite transparent. And within the pearl a huge red ruby kept spinning round and round, throwing out light that lit the whole hall, so it seemed as if the setting sun shone on it. And at the end of that great room Burd Ellen sat on a couch of velvet and gold. She was combing her golden hair with a silver comb, but looking sad, very sad. Up she sprang when she saw Chylde Roland. And she cried in a woeful voice:

"Oh my brother! My brother! God pity you! Why did you ever come here? Two brothers we've lost already! Why didn't you bide at home with our mother? For woe be unto you, if the King of Elfland finds you!"

"I came for you!" Chylde Roland cried.

" 'Twas useless. 'Twill be your death!" she answered. "But since you're here, come and sit ye down by my side!"

So the two sat down together and Burd Ellen told Chylde Roland all her sorry tale, how she herself was kept imprisoned here and how their brothers had been enchanted by the King of Elfland and were lying now in stone tombs in the cellar as if they had been dead. A long time these two talked, then Chylde Roland began to be hungry and, forgetting all about Merlin's warning, he asked for something to eat and drink.

Sadly Burd Ellen looked at him, for she knew what would happen to him if he ate a bite in that castle. After all, those other two brothers of hers had met the sad fate that had befallen them because they had failed to obey all the instructions Merlin had given them. But the Goblin King had put her under a spell so she could not speak out and warn Chylde Roland. She could only let her eyes speak for her and her pleading eyes he did not read. So rising, she left him and in time she returned with a loaf of bread and a golden bowl full of milk.

THROUGH FAIRY HALLS

Eagerly seizing the bowl, Chylde Roland had raised it to his lips, when suddenly he remembered all that Merlin had said. Before he had sipped a drop he dashed the bowl to the ground and cried, "Not a bite will I eat, not a drop will I sip in Elfland!"

As though in answer to those words of defiance, the two heard at that very moment an angry roaring and the stamping of feet coming down the passageway toward them. Then the Goblin King burst into the room, black and terrible and snorting fire.

Still all undaunted, Chylde Roland drew his good sword and rushed to meet the goblin.

"Strike if thou darest!" he cried.

But the goblin also brandished a sword in one of his claw-like hands. A wicked looking sword it was, for it sparked and flashed with an evil light and it swished through the air with a furious hiss like a snake about to strike. And as the goblin came raging

forward, he appeared to grow and grow in size, till he seemed nothing less than a giant. Bellowing, he leapt here and there, striking out at the youth with that sword, while poor Burd Ellen stood by, pale and speechless with fear for her brother.

But Chylde Roland bore that sword which had never been drawn save in a cause that was good and just, his father's sword which had never struck in vain. And there was no blow the goblin struck that Chylde Roland did not parry and turn aside.

For hours they fought. Then at last Chylde Roland pressed the goblin hard. With one mighty sweep of his sword, he sent the goblin's sword flying out of his claw and off to a distance where it fell to the floor dead and lifeless, no longer sparking and hissing. And now the goblin was on his knees, with Chylde Roland's sword pricking his throat. With a terrible scream he begged for his life.

"I'll grant thee thy life on one condition only!" Chylde Roland cried. "If thou wouldst not die by my sword, thou must release my sister from thy spells and raise my brothers to life!"

"Agreed!" the goblin said sullenly. And rising, he went to a chest from which he took a phial filled with a blood-red liquor, while Chylde Roland followed, pricking him with his sword to keep him at his task.

Then the goblin led Chylde Roland down to the cellar where stood a row of stone tombs. And as he opened two of these, the youth saw his brothers lying there, as though they had been dead. But when the King had anointed the ears, the eyelids, nostrils, lips, and finger-tips of the two they sprang at once into life.

After that the Elfin King said the words that disenchanted Burd Ellen. Then she and her three brothers went down the long passage and out of doors where they turned their backs on the Dark Tower forever. Happily they reached home, where the good Queen welcomed her children with the greatest joy. And Burd Ellen never went round a church "widershins" again.

THROUGH FAIRY HALLS
The Sleeping Beauty*

A LONG time ago there lived a King and Queen who said every day, "Ah, if only we had a child!" but for a long time they had no child to gladden them. So, when a beautiful little daughter was born, the King could scarcely contain himself for joy. He ordered a splendid feast to celebrate the event and he invited not only his friends, but also the fairies who give gifts to new-born children. There were thirteen such fairies in his kingdom, but the King was using gold plates to honor this special feast, and, as he had only twelve golden plates, he asked only twelve of these fairies, leaving the thirteenth uninvited.

Well, the feast was held with all splendor, and when it came to an end, the fairies bestowed their gifts on the baby. One gave her virtue; another, good nature; a third, wisdom; a fourth, beauty; and so on with everything that is good. But when eleven had

said their say, suddenly the thirteenth presented herself at the door. She was an ugly old woman whose gifts to children were always evil, so the father of little Briar-rose had done well to find no place for her at the feast. But now she forced her way into the hall in a fury to think she had not been invited, and went straight up to the baby's cradle.

"This is my gift to the King's daughter," she cried. "In her fifteenth year, she shall prick her finger with a spindle and die!" With these spiteful words, she stormed out of the hall.

*The beautiful *Sleeping Beauty Waltz* by the Russian composer, Tchaikovsky, is based on this old folk tale, which came, like "Cinderella" from the French book, *Tales of My Mother Goose* by Charles Perrault.

The King was left in terror, the Queen was in a panic, and the guests were struck dumb with fright. But just at that moment, the twelfth fairy stepped forward, for she had not yet made her promise for the child. "Nay," she said gently, "the Princess shall not die. She shall fall into a deep sleep."

Now the King was so anxious to guard his dear child from misfortune that he thought the best way would be to remove all spindles from his kingdom, and then she would never be able to prick her finger. So he gave orders, the very next day, that every spindle should be burned to ashes and never another one made.

Meanwhile, the gifts of the fairies were plenteously fulfilled in the little girl, for she was so beautiful, modest, and kind that all who saw her loved her. But it happened on the very day when she was fifteen years old, that the King and Queen, being now quite at rest about their daughter since they thought they had put all danger out of her reach, went away from home, leaving Briar-rose all alone. No sooner were they gone, than the Princess began to feel a great desire to go poking about the palace into all the strange places she had never visited before. So she went into all sorts of great, echoing halls and queer little chambers, and at last she came to an old stone tower, with a narrow stair that went winding upward. Up the rickety steps she started. She climbed and she climbed

THROUGH FAIRY HALLS

At last she came to a door with a queer, old rusty key in the lock. When she turned the key, the door sprang open. There, in a dusty little room, sat a little old woman in gray, and she was working busily.

"Good-day, my good dame," said Briar-rose, "what are you doing?"

"I am spinning," said the woman, nodding her head. And she drew out a thread of flax, twisting it deftly between her fingers.

"And what is that little thing you send twirling around there so very, very merrily?"

"A spindle! A spindle!"

"Ah!" cried little Briar-rose, "I have never seen anything merrier!" And she crept up closer and closer. At last, as she watched the twisting and twirling, she grew so anxious to try it herself that she said, "Good dame, pray let me try to spin."

At that the old woman smiled till the curves of her mouth went way up under her long hook-nose, then she handed Briar-rose the distaff and the spindle. The Princess tucked the distaff under her left arm as she had seen the old woman do, and started to pull out a thread. But alas! she knew nothing of spindles, nor had she ever been taught how to handle one properly. So, at the very first turn, she clumsily thrust the point into her hand and pricked her finger.

21

In an instant spindle and distaff dropped to the floor, little Briar-rose sank upon a bed and lay there in a deep sleep which spread over all the castle. Then the little old woman in gray disappeared and the room in the tower was quiet and still.

Down below, the King and Queen, who had just returned to the great hall of the castle, went to sleep on their thrones and all their courtiers with them. The horses went to sleep in their stables, the dogs went to sleep in the yard, the pigeons went to sleep on the roof, the flies went to sleep on the wall. Even the fire on the kitchen hearth stopped flaming and slept in its embers; the great iron kettle above left off boiling; and the cook, who was just going to pull the hair of a careless scullery boy, let him go and sank down fast asleep. The wind fell, the flowers and grasses sank down on the earth, and, on the trees before the castle, not a single leaf stirred again.

Round about the place, there began to grow a hedge of thorns; snow fell with ice and sleet. So many years passed by and every year the hedge grew denser and higher, till it hid every tower from sight. At last nothing at all could be seen of the castle, not even the flags on its roof. And over the spot, year in and year out, it was always frozen winter. But the story of the beautiful Princess, sleep-bound in her castle, still went abroad through the land.

From time to time the Kings' sons came determined to wake her. But they were so frightened at sight of that thorny hedge that they turned and fled. And the faster they ran the longer were the arms the hedge of thorns reached out to seize and destroy them. One and all, they were destroyed while Briar-rose slept on.

At last and at last, after many, many years, there came to the land a certain King's son to whom an old man told the tale of the Princess. He told the King's son how sadly the other Kings' sons had fared who tried to do battle with the hedge. But this youth said, "I am not afraid of the hedge. I shall go and awaken the beautiful Princess.

THROUGH FAIRY HALLS

The old man did all he could to dissuade the Prince from going, but the youth would not listen to his words. Off he set toward the frozen castle. As he drew near he felt its icy breath, he saw the snow over all and the giant thorn hedge that rose threateningly before him. But he was not afraid of that hedge as the other King's sons had been. Confidently he strode toward it and when he faced it squarely with such utter lack of fear, it suddenly turned green, blossomed with beautiful flowers and parted of its own accord to let him pass. Then the snow stopped falling and the ice melted. By the time he reached the castle yard all signs of winter had fled. The earth was in bloom about him. But the horses and dogs were still asleep, the pigeons on the rooftop still had their heads buried under their wings, and when he entered the castle the flies were still asleep on the wall, the fire slept in its embers, and the cook was still holding out her hand as though to cuff the scullery boy.

Within the great hall, the King and Queen lay asleep on their thrones with their whole court sleeping about them. All was so quiet everywhere that a breath could have been heard. At last the King's son came to the stone tower with the narrow stair that went winding upward. Up the rickety steps he climbed and opened the door of the little chamber.

There, before him on the bed, lay Briar-rose asleep. Her cheeks were faintly flushed, her hair was like gold, and her clothes were all quaint and old-fashioned, like those his great-great-grandmother had worn. So beautiful was she that the King's son could not turn his eyes from her. As he looked, he stooped down and gently gave her a kiss. The moment she felt his kiss, Briar-rose opened her eyes and awoke. Then she looked at him sweetly and slowly rose from her couch. Hand in hand, down the stairs together they went. When they entered the great hall of the castle, the King awoke and the Queen and the whole court, and all looked at each other astonished. The horses in the courtyard stood up and shook themselves, the dogs jumped up and wagged their tails, the pigeons on the roof awoke and flew away into open country, the flies on the wall crept again, the fire on the kitchen hearth flickered and flamed up, the great iron kettle began to boil, and the cook soundly boxed the ears of the scullery boy.

The very next day the marriage of the King's son with Briar-rose was celebrated with all rejoicing, and inside the castle and out was the life and bloom of the spring.

THROUGH FAIRY HALLS

THE ASSEMBLING OF THE FAYS

They come from beds of lichen green,
They creep from the mullein's velvet screen;
   Some on the backs of beetles fly
From the silver tops of moon-touched trees,
Where they swung in their cobweb hammocks high,
And rocked about in the evening breeze;
And now they throng the moonlight glade,
Above—below—on every side,
Their little minim forms arrayed,
In the tricksy pomp of fairy pride.

—*Joseph Rodman Drake*

25

The Good Comrades of the Flying Ship
A Russian Tale

THERE lived once upon a time in Russia a peasant and his wife, and they had three sons; two were clever, but the third was thought a fool. The elder brothers were forever telling him he had no wits, and he found himself always treated as of no use whatsoever. One day they all heard that a writing had come from the Tsar which said:

"Whoever builds a ship that can fly, to him will I give my daughter, the Tsarevna, to wife."

The elder brothers resolved to go and seek their fortune, and they begged a blessing of their parents. The mother got ready their things for the journey, and gave them the best she had in the house to eat on the way. Then the fool began to beg them to send him off too. His mother told him he should not go.

"Why shouldst thou go?" said his mother. "Dost thou think thou canst do what wiser men cannot?"

But the fool was always singing the same refrain, "I think I can! I want to go!"

At length his mother saw she could do nothing with him, so she gave him a poor crust of black bread and sent him out. The fool went and went, and at last he met an old man. They greeted each other, and the old man asked, "Where art thou going?"

"Look now," said the fool, "the Tsar has promised to give his daughter to him who shall make a flying ship!"

"And canst thou make such a ship?"

"No, I cannot, but I'll get it made for me somewhere."

"And where is that somewhere?"

"God only knows."

"Well, in that case, sit down here, rest and eat a bit. Share with me what thou hast in thy knapsack."

"Nay, it is such stuff that I am ashamed to share it with thee."

"Nonsense! Take it out! What God has given is quite good enough to be eaten."

The fool undid his knapsack and could hardly believe his eyes. There, instead of the dry crust of brown bread, lay white rolls and divers savory meats, and he gave of it to the old man. So they ate together and the old man said to the fool:

"Go into the wood, straight up to the first tree. Strike the trunk with thine axe, then fall with thy face to the ground and wait till thou art aroused. Thou wilt see before thee a ship quite ready. Sit in it and fly, and whomsoever thou dost meet on the road, gather him up and give him a lift on his journey."

So our fool blessed the old man, took leave of him, and went into the wood. He went up to the first tree and did exactly as he had been commanded. He struck the trunk with his axe, fell with his face to the ground and went to sleep. In a little while, something or other awoke him. The fool rose up and saw the ship quite ready beside him. Without loss of time, he got into it, and the ship flew up into the air. It flew and flew and look!—there on the road below a man was lying with his ear to the earth.

"Good day, uncle!" cried the fool.

"Good day!"

"What art thou doing?"

"I am listening to what is going on in the world."

"Art thou traveling?"

"Yea."

"Then take a seat in the ship beside me. I'll give thee a lift on thy journey."

So the man got into the ship and they flew on further. They flew and flew and look!—a man was coming along hopping on one leg, with the other leg tied tightly to his ear.

"Good day, uncle! Why art thou hopping on one leg?"

"Why, if I were to untie the other, I should stride around half the world at a single stride, so long are my steps!"

"Then take a seat in the ship beside me."

So the man got into the ship and they flew on further. They flew and flew and look!—a man was standing with a gun and taking aim, but at what they could not see.

"Good day, uncle, at what art thou aiming?"

"Oh, I'm aiming at a mark the size of a pea at a distance of one hundred leagues. That's what I call shooting!"

"Art thou traveling?"

"Yea!"

"Then take a seat in the ship beside me. I'll give thee a lift on thy journey."

So the man sat down and they flew on. They flew and flew and look!—a man was walking in the forest, and on his shoulders was a bundle of wood.

"Good day, uncle, why art thou dragging wood about?"

"Oh, but this is not common wood!"

"Of what sort is it, then?"

"It is of such a sort that if it be scattered, a whole army will spring up."

"Take a seat with us, then. I'll give thee a lift on thy journey."

So he also sat down with them and they flew on further. They flew and flew and look!—a man was carrying a sack of straw.

"Good day, uncle, whither art thou carrying that straw?"

"To the village."

"Is there little straw in the village, then?"

"Nay, but this straw is of such a kind that if it be scattered on the hottest summer day, cold will at once set in, with snow and frost."

THROUGH FAIRY HALLS

"Take a seat with us then. I'll give thee a lift on thy journey."

So they flew and flew and soon they flew into the Tsar's court-yard. The Tsar was sitting at table when he saw the flying ship drop from the sky just outside his window. In great surprise, he sent his servant to ask who it was that had accomplished the task.

The servant went to the ship and looked and brought back word to the Tsar that it was but a miserable little peasant who was flying the ship. The Tsar fell a-thinking. He did not wish to fulfill his promise by giving his daughter to a peasant, so he considered how he could rid himself of such a son-in-law.

"I will set him a task he can never perform," thought he.

Immediately he called his servant and bade him say to the fool: "Thou shalt get thy master, the Tsar, some of the living

and singing water from the other end of the world. And mind that thou bringest it here before the end of the meal which he is even now eating. Shouldst thou fail to do this, thou shalt pay for it with thy life."

Now at the very time when the Tsar was giving this command to his servant, the first comrade whom the fool had taken into the ship (that is to say Sharp-ear) heard what the Tsar said and told it to the fool.

"What shall I do now?" said the fool. "If I travel for my whole life I shall never get to the other end of the world, let alone bringing the water here before the imperial meal is over."

"Never fear," said Swift-of-foot, "I'll manage it for thee."

The servant came and made known the Tsar's commands.

"Say I'll fetch it," replied the fool, and Swift-of-foot untied his leg from his ear, ran off and in a twinkling was at the other end of the earth. There he got the living and singing water.

"I must make haste and return presently," said he, "but I've plenty of time for a nap first." And he sat down under a water-mill and went to sleep.

The Tsar's dinner was drawing to a close. He was eating dessert and was just putting his last sweetmeat to his lips, still Swift-of-foot did not turn up, so it appeared that all hope was lost for the fool. But Sharp-ear bent down to the earth and listened.

"Oh ho!" he cried, "Swift-of-foot has fallen asleep beneath the mill. I can hear him snoring."

Then Hit-the-mark seized his gun and fired a shot into the mill just above the sleeper's head. The noise awoke Swift-of-foot, who took one great stride and there he was back at the ship with the water. The Tsar was just ready to rise from the table, when the fool laid the water at his feet.

At this the Tsar was astounded. He saw he must think of

some other way to get rid of the fool, so he sent his servant to him and bade him prepare for his wedding.

"First go to the bath-room assigned thee, and have a good wash," he ordered.

Now this bath-room was made of cast-iron, and the Tsar commanded that it should be heated hotter than hot. So they heated the bath red hot. The fool went to wash himself, but when he drew near and felt the waves of heat that came forth from the door, he summoned the comrade with the straw.

"I must strew the floor," said the comrade. So both were locked into the bath-room, the comrade scattered the straw, the room at once became icy cold, and the water in the bath froze, so the fool could scarcely wash himself properly. He crept up onto the stove and there he passed the whole night.

In the morning servants opened the door of the bath and they found the fool alive and well, lying on the stove, and singing songs.

They brought word thereof to the Tsar. The Tsar was now sore troubled. He did not know how to get rid of the fool. He thought and thought, and at length he commanded the fool to produce a whole army of his own.

"How will a simple peasant be able to gather an army?" thought he. "He will surely fail this time."

The servant came to the fool and said: "If thou wilt have the Tsarevna, thou must, before morning, put a whole army on foot."

As soon as the fool heard this, he said to his comrades:

"You have delivered me from my straits more than once, my friends, but it is plain that nothing can be done now."

"Thou art a pretty fellow!" said the man with the bundle of wood. "Hast thou forgotten what I can do with my wood?"

So the fool took courage again and sent this word to the Tsar:

"I agree; I shall raise up the army our master, the Tsar,

demands of me. But tell him that should he again refuse to keep his word with me, I shall conquer his whole kingdom with the very army he bids me raise!"

At night the fool's companion went out into the fields, took his bundle of wood, and began scattering the fagots in different directions. Immediately a countless army sprang up, both horse and foot. In the morning the Tsar saw it, a multitude in arms, swarming over his whole country side, and then at last he cried:

"I am forced to yield; such an army as this could conquer my whole kingdom!"

So he sent in all haste to the fool with gifts of precious ornaments and raiment, and bade him come to be welcomed at court and married to the Tsarevna.

The fool attired himself in these costly garments. Then he richly repaid the friends who had proven such good comrades and was off to the Tsar. That same day he wedded the Tsarevna and lived henceforth with her at court. It now appeared that he was no fool at all, as men had thought him, but in truth a wise and clever young man. So the Tsar and Tsarevna grew very fond of him and it was soon his wisdom that was governing the kingdom.

JUDGING BY APPEARANCES★

EMILIE POULSSON

An old Jack-o'-lantern lay on the
   ground;
He looked at the Moon-man, yellow
   and round.

The old Jack-o'-lantern gazed and he
   gazed,
And still as he looked he grew more
   amazed.

Then said Jack-o'-lantern,
   "How can it be
That fellow up there looks so much
   like me?

"I s'pose he must be a brother of
   mine,
And somebody cut *him, too,* from the
   vine.

"He looks very grand up there in
   the sky;
But I know just how 'twill be, by
   and by.

"He's proud of his shining, I have
   no doubt,
But just wait until *his* candle goes
   out!"

★From *Through the Farmyard Gate.* Used by the courteous permission of Lothrop, Lee & Shepard Co.

MR. MOON*
BLISS CARMAN

O Moon, Mr. Moon,
When you comin' down?
Down on the hilltop,
Down in the glen,
Out in the clearin',
To play with little men?
Moon, Mr. Moon,
When you comin' down?

O Mr. Moon,
Hurry up your stumps!
Don't you hear Bullfrog
Callin' to his wife,
And old black Cricket
A-wheezin' at his fife?
Hurry up your stumps,
And get on your pumps!
Moon, Mr. Moon,
When you comin' down?

O Mr. Moon,
Hurry up along!
The reeds in the current
Are whisperin' slow;
The river 's a-wimplin'
To and fro.
Hurry up along,
Or you'll miss the song!
Moon, Mr. Moon,
When you comin' down?

O Mr. Moon,
We're all here!
Honey-bug, Thistledrift,
White-imp, Weird,
Wryface, Billiken,
Quidnunc, Queered;
We're all here,
And the coast is clear!
Moon, Mr. Moon,
When you comin' down?

O Mr. Moon,
There's not much time!
Hurry, if you're comin',
You lazy old bones!
You can sleep to-morrow
While the Buzbuz drones;
There's not much time
Till the church bells chime
Moon, Mr. Moon,
When you comin' down?

O Mr. Moon,
When you comin' down?
Down where the Good Folk
Dance in a ring,
Down where the Little Folk
Sing?
Moon, Mr. Moon,
When you comin' down?

A Midsummer Night's Dream

TOLD FROM THE PLAY BY WILLIAM SHAKESPEARE

ONCE there ruled in Athens a great and kindly Duke, who was just about to be married to a beautiful, young queen. All was jollity and merriment throughout the countryside in making ready for their wedding. But while everyone was so happy, there came before the Duke, Egeus, a stern old graybeard, dragging his daughter with him and followed by two young men.

"Most noble lord!" he said. "This rebellious maiden, Hermia, my daughter, will not wed Demetrius here, the youth I've chosen for her! She vows she'll wed this other youth, Lysander! He hath bewitched her! Stolen her heart! No more will she obey me! So, gracious Duke," the old man's voice rose angrily, "I now demand that, in accordance with the law of Athens, you sentence my daughter to die if she will not obey my commands!"

"But, noble lord!" poor Hermia pleaded. "I do not love Demetrius! 'Tis Lysander that I love!"

"And this Demetrius, what sort of man is he?" Lysander cried. "He loves no maid for long! Until but recently he loved Helena, Hermia's friend, who is devoted to him still."

But Hermia's stern old father continued to insist that the Duke should carry out the law. The Duke was much distressed. He sympathized with the lovers, Hermia and Lysander, but against the law of the land he could do nothing at all. Therefore, he had to declare that Hermia should have four days in which to consider the matter. If, at the end of that time, she still refused to wed Demetrius, then Hermia must die.

THROUGH FAIRY HALLS

Exulting at this decision, Demetrius and Egeus soon went off with the Duke who begged them to confer with him on matters concerning his wedding. Thus Lysander was left alone with the sad and weeping Hermia. And he said to her with spirit:

"Hermia, O my Hermia! The course of true love never did run smooth! But hearken unto me! I have an aunt who lives out in the country far enough from this city so the cruel law of Athens cannot be enforced there. Tomorrow night at moonrise, steal from thy father's house. In that deep wood where I did meet thee once with Helena, to do observance to a morn of May, there I will wait for thee. Together we will flee to the home of my good aunt."

Joyfully Hermia agreed to do as Lysander asked. The next day she made ready to flee from the city and she told no one of her plans except her old friend Helena.

"Take comfort, Helena!" she said. "I'll never marry thy Demetrius. Tonight I'm leaving Athens in secret to wed Lysander."

But Helena was distracted with the grief which she had suf-fered through unkindness of De-metrius. Thinking only of gaining favor with him, she went that evening and told him that Hermia had fled. Demetrius was furious. Cruelly he berated Helena and he set out at once to seek Hermia, while Helena followed him, vainly trying to win a word of kindness.

Meantime, Hermia and Ly-sander had met. Arms about each other, they were wandering through the woods on their way to the house of Lysander's aunt, feeling happy and safe at last.

Now in this same shadowy, silvery, moonlit midsummer
wood—unseen by all four lovers—a train of little elves held their
midnight revels. They flitted through the groves in the spangled
sheen of the starlight; they gamboled on the greens and hung
dewdrops in the cowslip's ears. Of these little elves, Oberon
was the King and Titania the Fairy Queen.

But unhappily, at this time, Oberon and Titania had quarreled
with one another. Whenever the fairies danced by fountain,
brook, or seashore, Oberon and Titania stormed with such rage at
each other that all their tiny elves crept into acorn cups and
hid themselves for fear.

The reason for this quarrel was that Titania had taken a
little human boy, whose mother was dead. Titania had loved the
mother and now she coddled the boy. She pampered, petted,

spoiled him, keeping him always a baby, while Oberon wished to take him and make him into a page to serve as his attendant among his merry train of jolly little boy-elves. On that very midsummer night, when the lovers wandered in the wood, it chanced that Oberon met Titania, attended by some of her fairies.

"Ill met by moonlight, proud Titania!" cried the Fairy King.

"Jealous Oberon, is it you?" Titania tossed her head. "Fairies, skip hence! I will have none of his company."

"How dare you cross me?" stormed Oberon. "Give me that boy for my page."

"Not all your Fairy Kingdom shall buy that boy from me!" Titania left the King in anger.

"Go your way!" cried Oberon. "But ere the morning dawns I will torment you for this wrong."

And straightway he thought up a plan to play such a trick on Titania that she would wish to give that human boy into his keeping. Then he summoned Puck, the most impish of all his elves. A clever but mischievous sprite was Puck. In all the neighboring villages, he had played comical pranks. Sometimes, when a few good neighbors were cozily met together to gossip and drink their ale, Puck would plump himself, in the likeness of a roasted crab apple, into a mug of ale; and just as some worthy old woman was lifting the mug to drink, he would bob up against her lips, and spill the ale over her chin. And when that same old dame had gravely started to tell some lengthy tale, he would seize her three-legged stool and suddenly pull it out from under her. Then the poor old lady would topple down on the floor in such a ridiculous heap, that the gossips held their sides with laughter. If there was any of Oberon's elves who knew all about mischievous tricks it was Puck.

"Puck," Oberon said to this sprite, "go now through the woods and bring me back that flower which maidens call Love-in-Idleness. The juice of that little blossom, if it is squeezed on the eyelids of anyone asleep will make that person, on waking, dote on the first thing he sees. Some of the juice I'll drop on the eyelids of my Titania and whatever she sees when she wakes, she will fall

madly in love with—be it a bear or a
tiger, a meddling monkey, or a busy ape!
And before I remove this charm, I will make
her give me that boy to be my page."

Delighted to mix in such mischief, Puck cut
a little caper. "I'll put a girdle round the earth
in forty minutes!" he cried. And off he dashed like a streak.

But while Oberon waited in the wood for Puck to return with
the flower, he chanced—all unseen himself—to see Helena and
Demetrius wandering beneath the trees. Cruelly the young Athenian was shouting at the gentle maiden: "Leave me! Leave me!
'Tis Hermia I seek! 'Tis Hermia I love! And if thou wilt not
leave me, I'll leave thee! Leave thee to the mercy of
the wild beasts in this forest!" Then he ran off into
the woods while Helena, crying out in grief
and terror, tried to follow him into
the darkness.

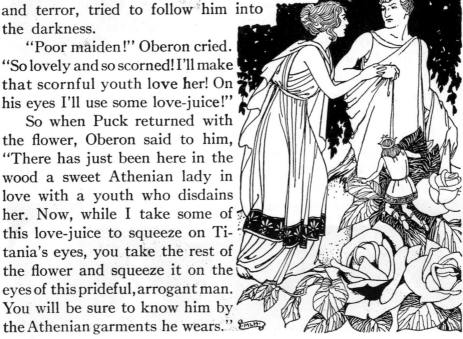

"Poor maiden!" Oberon cried.
"So lovely and so scorned! I'll make
that scornful youth love her! On
his eyes I'll use some love-juice!"

So when Puck returned with
the flower, Oberon said to him,
"There has just been here in the
wood a sweet Athenian lady in
love with a youth who disdains
her. Now, while I take some of
this love-juice to squeeze on Titania's eyes, you take the rest of
the flower and squeeze it on the
eyes of this prideful, arrogant man.
You will be sure to know him by
the Athenian garments he wears."

"Fear not, my lord," said Puck. "Your servant will do as you say." And he darted away to obey the commands of Oberon, while the King, himself, went off to find the Fairy Queen.

Now, at some time of the night, Titania always slept on a mossy green bank where the wild thyme grew amid cowslips and nodding violets. Beneath a thick, sheltering canopy of roses and woodbine vines, Titania would sleep in a blossom, cozily wrapped in a glittering, gaily-enameled snakeskin and gently rocked by the wind as if she had been in a cradle. As Oberon crept up quietly to this beautiful bower of Titania's, he heard her ordering her fairies what to do while she slept.

"Some of you go," she said, "to kill the cankerworms that eat the musk-rose buds! Some wage war with bats, and get their leathern wings to make my small elves coats; and some of you keep watch that the clamorous old owl, who nightly hoots in the forest, come not near my cradle. But first, fairies, sing me to sleep."

So the fairies started to sing—

"*You spotted snakes with double tongue,*
Thorny hedgehogs, be not seen!
Newts and blindworms do no wrong,
Come not near our Fairy Queen!
Philomel, with melody,
Sing in our sweet lullaby,
Lulla, lulla, lullaby; lulla, lulla, lullaby;
Never harm, nor spell, nor charm,
Come our lovely lady nigh;
So good night with lullaby."

And when Titania had fallen asleep, the elves and fairies all flew away to do as she had bidden them leaving the Queen alone. So Oberon, drawing near her softly, squeezed on her eyelids some of his magic love-juice. Then he was off to the woods to wait what should come to pass.

Meanwhile Puck went skipping, leaping, bounding through the forest in search of that Athenian to whom Oberon had directed him. At length he saw before him a youth and maiden sleeping in the night and silence.

"Here's my man!" he cried. "He wears Athenian garments." And he ran up to the youth and squeezed the juice of the flower on the closed eyes of the sleeper. Then off he ran well-content that he had performed his task.

But Puck alas, had made a sad mistake. He had squeezed the juice, not on the eyes of Demetrius, but on the sleeping Lysander, and the lady lying near was not the sad Helena, but Lysander's beloved, Hermia.

Wandering through the wood toward the home of Lysander's aunt, the lovers had grown so weary that they had lain down to sleep. And now as they lay there peacefully, the unhappy, deserted Helena, still seeking Demetrius through the night and the darkness of the forest, came into the little glade, forlorn and all alone. Stumbling on Lysander's form lying so still on the grass, she stopped in great surprise; for Hermia lay so far away that Helena did not see her hidden in the shadows.

"What does Lysander here? Is he dead or asleep?" Touching him gently, she said, "Lysander, if you live, awake!"

So Lysander, opening his eyes, saw first of all fair Helena. At once the love-juice worked. He, who so loved Hermia, now, through Puck's mistake, believed that he loved only Helena.

"Sweet Helena," he cried. "How fair I see thee now! How could I ever have believed 'twas Hermia I loved? 'Tis thee I love, my Helena!"

THROUGH FAIRY HALLS

Then Helena was astounded. She thought Lysander mocked her. She did not believe that he loved her and, as he persisted in speaking a lover's words in her ears, she tried to escape him in flight; but Lysander followed her pleading. Thus when Hermia awoke a few moments later, she found herself alone.

"Lysander!" she cried. "Lysander! Where are you?" And since he did not answer she set out, sick with fear, to find him.

But Puck, all unaware of the mischief he had wrought, went merrily on his way to provide some ridiculous object for Titania to fall in love with when she awoke. Soon he found near the place where she slept some loutish simpletons from the city who had come out into the woods to practice for a play they meant to present for the Duke during his wedding festivities. There was Quince, the carpenter; Snug, the joiner; Flute, a bellows-mender; Snout, a tinker; Starveling, a tailor; and Bottom, the weaver.

"One of these ninnies should make an absurd enough lover!" Puck chuckled. Then he chuckled again as he heard how sad was the play with which they meant to make the Duke merry. It was all about Thisby, a maiden whose parents shut her up in a place surrounded by a high wall so she could not marry Pyramus, her lover. Going by moonlight to talk to her lover through a hole in the wall, Thisby was frightened away by a lion, so Pyramus, finding only her cloak stained with blood from the lion's jaws, thought the lion had slain her and stabbed himself to death.

"Nick Bottom," said Quince, the carpenter, who was directing the play, "you must be Pyramus, the lover, who kills himself most gallantly for love."

"Aye!" Bottom boasted. "I will play the lover so I move a storm of tears! Let the audience look to their eyes! But yet the ladies will not like that. 'Twill fright them to see a man killed. There must come a man on the stage to explain that this Pyramus is not really killed, since I am not really Pyramus but only Bottom, the weaver."

"So be it," said Quince. "And you, Flute, must play Thisby."

"O let me be Thisby, too!" Bottom squeaked in a thin little voice. "I'll speak in a monstrous little voice just fit for a lady."

"No," said Quince. "You can play no part but Pyramus. And Snug, you shall play the lion. All you have to do is roar."

"Let me play the lion, too!" Bottom wanted all the parts. "I will roar so that it will do any man's heart good to hear me. I will roar so that I will make the Duke say, 'Roar again!'"

46

"But if you roared too terribly, you would fright all the ladies!" Quince scratched his head, perplexed. "And that were enough to hang us!"

"Then I will roar gently, gently, as gently as a dove," cooed Bottom. "I will roar like a nightingale."

"You can play only Pyramus!" Quince insisted stubbornly.

"But masters," said Bottom, "you ought to consider with yourselves that to bring in a lion among ladies is a most dreadful thing, for there is not a more fearful wild fowl than your lion living. If Snug is to play the lion, let him show his face through the lion's neck and he must speak through thus: 'Ladies—or fair ladies—I would wish you—or I would request you—or I would entreat you—not to fear—not to tremble. If you think I come hither as a lion, it were pity of my life. No, I am no such thing; I am a man as other men are.' And there, let him name his name and tell them plainly he is Snug, the joiner."

"It shall be so," said Quince. "But there be still two things I know not how to do—to bring moonlight onto the stage and, likewise, to bring in a wall for the lovers to whisper through. Mayhap for the moon, a man might come in with a lantern and say he represents moonshine; but what shall we do for a wall?"

"That's easy!" Bottom was sure he knew everything. "Some man must represent Wall. Let him have some plaster or bits of clay hanging to him, and let him hold his fingers up to represent the hole for the lovers to whisper through."

"If that may be, all is well!" Quince nodded his approval. "Now let us rehearse our parts. Bottom, you begin."

Swaggering importantly, Bottom spoke up while Puck laughed to himself, "Of all these hempen homespuns swaggering here, 'tis Bottom who'll make the most absurd lover for Titania!"

Having spoken his part on the little stretch of greensward being used for a stage, Bottom now retired to some bushes, which served as the dressing-room. Then Puck, by his magic, turned Bottom's head into an ass's head. And the poor simpleton, knowing nothing of the change that had been wrought in him, strutted back to the stage wearing the ass's head and loudly braying his next line, "Fair Thisby, I love thee! Heehaw! Heehaw!"

"Oh monstrous! We're haunted! Murder! Help!" cried his friends, and they took to their heels and ran away in terror.

"Why do they run away? This is a knavery of them to make me afeared," said Bottom. "This is to make an ass of me! To fright me if they could! But I'll walk up and down and sing, that they shall hear I'm not afraid!" And as Bottom walked off, singing, his voice awakened Titania. Straightway the love-juice worked. She looked on the lumbering lout with his long-eared ass's head and she thought him as beautiful as an angel.

"What angel wakes me from my flowery bed?" she said.

Still heehawing, Bottom went on braying nonsense—

> *"The finch, the sparrow and the lark.*
> *The plain song cuckoo grey*
> *Whose note full many a man doth mark*
> *And dares not answer nay!"*

Yet to Titania that seemed the loveliest song in the world. Slipping down from her cradle in the blossom she cried:

"I pray thee, gentle mortal, sing again!"

Then she led the ridiculous, hairy, ass-headed monster to her flowery bank and made him sit beside her. She twined his clumsy head with fragrant pink musk-roses and other delicate flowers and she stroked his long, fuzzy ears.

"Thou art as wise as thou art beautiful," she said. "I will give thee fairies to attend on thee. They shall fetch thee jewels from the deep and sing while thou dost sleep on a bed of fragrant blossoms. I'll make of thee an airy spirit. Come Peaseblossom, Cobweb, Moth, and Mustardseed!" She called her elves and fairies. "Feed him with apricots and dewberries, with purple grapes, green figs, and mulberries. Steal honey bags from the bumblebees. Take their wax for candles and light them at the glowworm's eyes to light my love to bed and to arise. Bring wings from the painted butter-flies to fan the moonbeams from his sleeping eyes. Nod to him elves, and do him courtesies."

Lightly Peaseblossom, Mustardseed and other elves, named for fairylike flowers, came tripping forward. But Bottom knew nothing of fairylike flowers. He knew only big fat vegetables. "Good Master Peaseblossom," he roared, "commend me to Mistress Squash, your mother, and Master Peasecod, your father.

And you Master Mustardseed,
I know peppery cousins of yours
that have made my eyes smart ere now!"
   Then, finding it much to his liking
to have all these servants to order about,
he bellowed, "Peaseblossom, scratch my head! Methinks
I am marvelous hairy about the face, and I am such a tender ass;
if my hair do but tickle me, I must always scratch. Cobweb,
bring bags from the honey bees! And you, Mustardseed, you
help Peaseblossom to scratch."
   "Will you have music, my sweet love?" Titania whispered.

51

"Aye! I like music!" Bottom blared. "Heehaw! Heehaw! Let's have a good clatter of the tongs and the bones!"

"Or say, love, what thou desirest to eat." Titania urged. "Shall it be the dewberries, the mulberries or the grapes?"

"I could munch your good dry oats!" Bottom rumbled. "And methinks I have a great desire for hay, good hay, sweet hay."

"I have a venturesome fairy that shall seek the squirrel's hoard and fetch thee nuts!" Titania's voice was silvery as a bell.

"I had rather have a handful or two of dried peas," boomed Bottom. "But I have an exposition of sleep come upon me. I pray you let me sleep, and let none of your people disturb me." So he drifted off into slumber while Titania held his head.

To Puck, looking on in secret, all this was a merry joke. Off he ran and told Oberon of the monster Titania now loved. But as the two laughed together, they saw coming toward them Hermia, who was all forlorn because she could not find Lysander. And with her was Demetrius, whom she had met while she was seeking her own true love.

"Why dost thou rebuke me when I love thee so?" Demetrius mourned, walking as close as he could by Hermia's side.

"O leave me!" cried Hermia. "Thou drivest me past all bounds of patience! Hast thou slain my Lysander! Where, O where is he?"

Then Oberon was astonished. "What hast thou done!" he cried to Puck. "This is the youth on whom I bade thee use the juice of our magic flower. But this is not the maiden with whom he should be in love!"

"Then there must be two Athenian youths in these woods," Puck answered. "For this is not the youth on whose eyes I squeezed the juice. But this is the maid who was with that youth!"

"Alas!" cried Oberon. "Then thou hast laid the love-juice on some true lover's sight."

But now as Hermia, in her anger, flounced off into the woods, Demetrius, discouraged and worn out, lay down and fell asleep.

THROUGH FAIRY HALLS

"Go swifter than the wind about the wood," said Oberon to Puck, "and make good thy mistake. Find Helena of Athens. All pale and sad she looks. See that thou bringest her here while I squeeze the magic love-juice on this Athenian's eyes."

With a leap, Puck bounded off, crying:

> *"I go, I go; look how I go*
> *Swifter than arrow from the Tartar's bowl!"*

In a moment more he was back, his errand performed, and he said to Oberon gleefully, "Captain of our fairy band, Helena is near at hand! And the youth, mistook by me, pleading for a lover's fee! Lord, what fools these mortals be!"

Then he laughed impishly at the mix-up caused by his mistake. For he knew that when Demetrius awoke, both he and Lysander, having the love-juice in their eyes, would now be wooing the once scorned Helena since Hermia was nowhere in sight.

In another instant Helena appeared with Lysander tagging after her, begging for her love. And their voices awoke Demetrius. Rising, Demetrius cried, "Helena, my love, my goddess!" Then he, too, began to woo Helena. In a few moments more, he and Lysander were shouting furiously at each other. Then, to make matters worse, Hermia, hearing her lover's voice, came up and joined the group, bewildered to find her true love now wooing another maid. Soon she and Helena fell to bitter quarreling also.

"You cankerworm!" Hermia shrieked to Helena. "You thief of love! You stole my Lysander!"

"You little puppet! You doll! You dwarf!" Helena shrieked back.

"So you'd twit me with being short of stature!" Hermia blazed. "You, you big, tall, painted maypole!"

Meantime, Demetrius and Lysander, shouting wildly and growing ever angrier, made off from the spot. Leaving the screeching maidens, they went chasing off into the depths of the forest to fight out with their fists their jealous quarrel over Helena.

"Hurry, Puck!" Oberon commanded. "Overcast the night with fog that these two youths may not see each other. Lead them apart with tricks. Pretend to be Lysander first, saying taunting words to Demetrius; and when Demetrius follows thee, thinking thou art Lysander, lead him far off from Lysander. Then do the same with Lysander. And when thou hast separated the two, squeeze the juice from this other magic flower on Lysander's eyes, so he shall love Hermia as before. But leave Demetrius as he is. Thus to all four lovers what's happened tonight will seem to have been a mere midsummer night's dream."

Bounding off Puck cried:

"Jack shall have Jill
Naught shall go ill,
The man shall have his mare again and all shall go well."

But Oberon went back to deal with Titania. And now the dainty little Queen so doted on the great clumsy ass-headed monster, that she willingly gave to Oberon the little boy she had spoiled with coddling—the cause of all their quarrels. And Oberon sent the child off to join his train of boy-elves. Then, filled with pity for his Queen, he squeezed the healing juice on her eyes the moment she fell asleep, speaking this magic charm:

"Be as thou wast wont to be,
See as thou wast wont to see."

And gently touching Titania, he woke her from her sleep.

"Wake you, my Titania! Wake you, my Queen!" he cried.

"Oberon!" Titania opened her eyes and looked at Oberon as though she had never really seen him before. "My Oberon, what a dream have I had! Methought I loved an ass!"

"There lies your love," said Oberon pointing to the sleeping Bottom who was snoring away at a great pace.

"How came these things to pass? How I do loathe him now!" Titania looked with disgust at Bottom.

"Think no more of the matter! 'Tis ended!" said Oberon. And as Puck at that moment returned from straightening out the tangle which he had made for the lovers, Oberon said to him:

"Puck, take the ass's head straightway off that sleeping bumpkin! Titania and I will go our way in new happiness. No more will we quarrel or frighten our elves and fairies when they dance within the woodland. Tomorrow night we will go to the wedding of the Duke. We will bless him and his house and these four lovers we have united."

So while Oberon and Titania went off happily together, Puck went over to Bottom and removed the ass's head. Then he ran away himself into the depths of the forest.

Soon Bottom awoke all confused. "I have had a dream past the wit of man to say what dream it was," he mumbled. "Methought I was—there is no man can tell what! And methought I had—but man is a fool if he offers to say what methought I had. The eye of man hath not heard, the ear of man hath not seen, man's hand is not able to taste, his tongue to conceive, or his heart report, what my dream was. I will get Peter Quince to write a ballad of my dream; and it shall be called, 'Bottom's Dream' because it hath no bottom!"

And off went the simpleton to boast to Snug and Snout and Quince and Starveling and all the rest of his friends, of the marvelous, unspeakable wonders that had befallen him that night.

The next evening, all was gaiety in the Duke's palace. Three weddings were now to be celebrated; not only the marriage of the Duke and his beautiful Duchess, but the marriage of Hermia and Lysander, of Helena and Demetrius, too, for the lovers had returned together in joy and peace to Athens, their troubles all forgotten. And Hermia's stern old father, being informed that Demetrius no longer wanted his daughter, was obliged to give his consent to Hermia's wedding Lysander. Thus all was merriment and happiness at the outcome of so many tangled affairs.

Bottom and his friends gave their play before the lovers. Roars of laughter greeted them with shouts of "Well roared, lion! Well shone, moon! Well stabbed, Pyramus!" And when the festivities ended and the lights had been put out, the elves and fairies came lightly tripping to bless the three couples in the house.

THROUGH FAIRY HALLS

Puck crept in cautiously first and seeing no humans there, he began blithely to sing:

"We fairies that do run
From the presence of the sun,
Following darkness like a dream
Now are frolic! Not a mouse
Shall disturb this hallowed house.
I am sent with broom before
To sweep the dust behind the door."

After him came all the fairies, swarming about like fireflies and Oberon sang gaily:

"By the dead and drowsy fire
Every elf and fairy sprite
Hop as light as bird from brier!
Now shall all these couples three
Ever true in loving be!"

Taking his hand, Titania answered:

"Hand in hand with fairy grace
We will sing and bless the place."

And that was the end of the midsummer night's dream.

A Musical Visit to Fairyland

A STORY OF FELIX MENDELSSOHN (1809–1847)

FELIX MENDELSSOHN had a sister named Fanny. The two always played together and Felix loved Fanny more than anyone else in the world. They lived in Germany, in a large home with blooming gardens and plenty of room to romp in, for their father was a rich banker. Both children loved the piano standing in its big room, so shiny and beautiful; and, among the many games they played, the one they loved best of all was a guessing game they had invented to play on that piano.

When Felix went out in the woods or strolled about the city among the other boys, leaving Fanny alone at home, he told his sister as soon as he returned what interesting things he had seen on his adventures of the day. But he did not tell her in words.

THROUGH FAIRY HALLS

He sat down at the piano and swiftly made up some music to describe what he had seen. Then Fanny had to guess what it was that her brother was telling about in the music he was playing.

One day, he sat down and ran his fingers over the keys. There, as if by magic, came the rousing call of a bugle. Then with a boom, boom, boom, the boy drummed on the lower notes.

"You saw a company of soldiers marching through the streets with their band," Fanny promptly guessed.

On another day Felix played high up on the upper keys, a little air with many trills rollicking gaily through it.

"You were out in the woods," said Fanny, "and you heard a bird sing like that!"

So that was how Felix began to make up songs without words. One day when Felix was seventeen, he and Fanny were sitting out in the garden of the house where they lived—at that time in Berlin. They were reading a book together; and it chanced to be Shakespeare's play, "A Midsummer Night's Dream," for the Mendelssohn family intended to give that play soon for their friends. Regularly musicians, artists, sculptors, poets, and actors gathered at the home of the Mendelssohn's to have a good time together; so the family was now planning to entertain their guests by presenting this merry play. How the young people enjoyed the delicate tale of the fairies—of Oberon, the Fairy King; Titania, the Fairy Queen; and that mischievous little sprite, Puck! And how they laughed at the clowns and all the ridiculous antics of Bottom when he was bewitched and wearing the ass's head!

"Why don't you write some music about those clowns and the fairies?" Fanny suggested to Felix.

Full of the story, the youth went off and set to work. After a time, he eagerly called Fanny to come and hear the music he had composed. Four magic chords and Fanny was off to Fairyland. The girl was delighted with the music. She wanted Felix to play it when they gave the play at the house.

The piece was an overture to be given before the play started. But, when all the audience gathered, Felix did not play alone, as he had before on his piano, for friends had brought violins, horns, bassoons, and other instruments, and it was now a whole orchestra that played the Overture.

The company was enchanted just as Fanny had been. Those same four magic chords and all the friends gathered there were off to Fairyland. Busily tripping, the music told all about the fairies; light, airy, tinkling notes—brimming with fun and frolic. Sparkling, delicate, dainty, it was full of the bustle of elves with a little pixie note of mischief when Puck came in on the scene. Then it grew dignified, stately, and there were the Duke and his court. But now it burst out intensely into deep strains of feeling and there were the poor young lovers all mixed up in their hearts by the crazy mistake of Puck. Then hee-haw, there was Bottom with all his rustic followers. The orchestra's clowns, the bassoons, the bass of the wood-wind choir were booming and squeaking grotesquely—leaping with great agility all up and down the scale and issuing in a droll dance with a succession of clownish antics. There was even the braying of Bottom, strutting in his ass's head. And once more at the close, there were the fairies again and those four magic chords dissolving the pretty dream.

What applause greeted Felix when the Overture was finished! His setting for the fairy comedy had reflected the changing feelings, as the merry drama progressed, better than many an opera tells its story with its music. And so popular did this Overture become in time in Germany, that many years later, the King hearing an orchestra play it, begged Felix to finish his work. So Felix went back with enthusiasm to "A Midsummer Night's Dream" and completed the music for it. The wedding march he composed for the marriage of the Duke was so majestic and stately, so beautiful and imposing, that to this very day, it is

played at nearly all weddings. Almost all brides and grooms walk out of church today to the strains of Mendelssohn's "Wedding March," which was written for the Duke and the fairies in "A Midsummer Night's Dream." And Mendelssohn's chief claim to fame rests on the graceful music, so full of melodic charm, which he wrote for Shakespeare's play and which he began to compose when he was only a boy.

Daniel O'Rourke

ADAPTED FROM T. CROFTON CROKER

PEOPLE may have heard of the renowned adventures of Daniel O'Rourke, but few there be who know that the cause of all his perils, above and below, was neither more nor less than his having slept under the walls of the Pooka's Tower. An old man was he at the time he told me the story, with gray hair and a red nose; he sat smoking his pipe under the old poplar tree, on as fine an evening as ever shone from the sky.

"I am often *axed* to tell it, sir," said he. "The master's son you see, had come from beyond foreign parts in France and Spain as young gentlemen used to do, and, sure enough, there was a dinner given to all the people on the ground, gentle and simple, high and low, rich and poor.

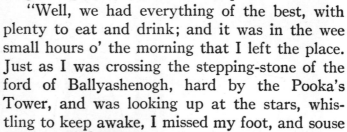

"Well, we had everything of the best, with plenty to eat and drink; and it was in the wee small hours o' the morning that I left the place. Just as I was crossing the stepping-stone of the ford of Ballyashenogh, hard by the Pooka's Tower, and was looking up at the stars, whistling to keep awake, I missed my foot, and souse I fell into the water. '*Begorra!*' thought I. 'Is it drounded I'm goin' to be?' However, I began swimming, swimming, swimming away for dear life, till at last I got ashore, somehow or other, but never the one of me can tell how, on a *desarted* island.

62

THROUGH FAIRY HALLS

"I wandered and wandered about, without knowing where I wandered, until at last I got into a big bog. The moon was shining as bright as day, and I looked east and west, north and south, and every way, and nothing did I see but bog, bog, bog. So I sat upon a stone, and I began to scratch my head for, sure and certain, thinks I, here's the end o' Daniel O'Rourke. And I began to sing the *Ullagone*—when, all of a sudden, the moon grew black, and I looked up and saw something for all the world as if it was moving down between me and it, and I could not tell what it was. Down it came with a pounce and looked me full in the face, and what was it but an eagle?—as fine a one as ever flew from the kingdom of Kerry. So he looked me in the face, and says he, 'Daniel O'Rourke,' says he, 'how do you do?'

" 'Very well, I thank you, sir,' says I, 'I hope you're well'; wondering out of my senses all the time how an eagle came to speak like a Christian.

" 'What brings you here, Dan?' says he.

" 'Nothing at all, sir,' says I, 'only I wish I was safe home again.'

" 'Is it out of the bog you want to go, Dan?' says he.

" ' 'Tis, sir,' says I.

" 'Dan,' says he, after a minute's thought, 'as you are a decent sober man, who never flings stones at me or mine, my life for yours,' says he, 'get up on my back, grip me well, and I'll fly you out of the bog.'

" 'I am afraid,' says I, 'your honour's making game of me, for whoever heard of riding a-horseback on an eagle before?'

" ' 'Pon the honour of a gentleman,' says he, putting his right foot on his breast, 'I am quite in earnest, and so now

Love and fun characterize Irish stories, dances and music. The most popular Irish dance is the jig. *The Galway Piper* and *Top o' Cork Road* are jolly old Irish airs.

either take my offer or starve in the bog!'

"I had no choice; so, thinks I to myself, faint heart never won fair lady. 'I thank your honour,' says I, 'for the kind offer.' I therefore mounted on the back of the eagle and held him tight enough by the throat, and up he flew in the air like a lark. Little I knew the trick he was going to serve me. Up, up, up—God knows how far he flew. 'Why, then,' said I to him—thinking he did not know the right road home—very civilly, because why? I was in his power entirely. 'Sir,' says I, 'please your honour's glory, and with humble submission to your better judgment, if you'd fly down a bit, you're now just over my cabin, and I could be put down there, and many thanks to your worship.'

" '*Arrah*, Dan,' says he, 'do you think me a fool? Hold your tongue, and mind your own business, and don't be interfering with the business of other people.'

" 'Faith, this is my business, I think,' says I. 'Where in the world are you going, sir?'

" 'Be quiet, Dan!' says he, and *bedad* he flew on and on.

"Well sir, where should we come to at last but to the moon, itself. Now you can't see it from here, but there is, or there was in my time, a reaping-hook sticking out of the side of the moon.

" 'Dan,' says the eagle, 'I'm tired with this long fly. I had no notion 'twas so far!'

" 'And my lord, sir," says I, 'who in the world *axed* you to fly so far—was it I? Did not I beg and pray and beseech you to stop half an hour ago?'

" 'There's no use talking, Dan,' said he, 'I'm tired so you must get off, and sit down on the moon until I rest.'

" 'Is it sit down upon that little round thing?' said I. 'Why then, sure, I'd fall off in a minute and be split and smashed entirely. You are a vile deceiver, so you are.'

" 'Not at all, Dan,' says he. 'You can catch fast hold of the reaping-hook that's sticking out of the side of the moon, and 'twill keep you up.'

" 'I won't then,' said I.

" 'Maybe not,' said he, quite quiet. 'If you don't, my man, I shall just give you a shake, and one slap of my wing, and send you down smash to the ground!'

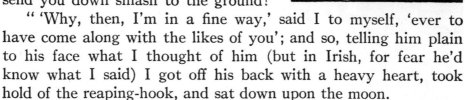

" 'Why, then, I'm in a fine way,' said I to myself, 'ever to have come along with the likes of you'; and so, telling him plain to his face what I thought of him (but in Irish, for fear he'd know what I said) I got off his back with a heavy heart, took hold of the reaping-hook, and sat down upon the moon.

"When he had me there fairly landed, he turned about on me and said, 'Good morning to you, Daniel O'Rourke,' said he. 'I think I've nicked you fairly now. You robbed my nest last year and in return, you are freely welcome to cool your heels dangling upon the moon.'

" 'Is this how you leave me, you brute, you?' says I. 'You ugly, urnatural *baste!*' 'Twas all to no manner of use. He spread out his great wings, burst out a-laughing, and flew away like lightning. I bawled after him to stop, but I might have called and bawled forever, without his minding me. Away he went, and I never saw him from that day to this. You may be sure I was in a disconsolate condition and kept roaring out for the bare grief, when, all at once, a door opened right in the middle of the moon, creaking on its hinges as if it had not been opened for a month before—I suppose they never thought of greasing them—and out there walks—who do you think but the man in the moon himself? I knew him by his bush.

" 'Good morrow to you, Daniel O'Rourke,' says he, 'how do you do?'

" 'Very well, thank your honour,' says I. 'I hope your honour finds yourself very well.'

" 'What brought you here, Dan?' said he. So I told him all the whole of the terrible story.

" 'Dan,' said the man in the moon, calmly taking a pinch of snuff, 'you must not stay here.'

" 'Indeed, sir,' says I, ' 'tis much against my will that I'm here at all, but how am I to go back?'

" 'That's your business,' said he. 'Dan, my business is to tell you that you must not stay where you are, so be off in less than no time.'

" 'I'm doing no harm,' said I, 'only holding on hard by this reaping-hook here lest I fall off.'

" 'That's what you must not do, Dan,' says he.

" 'Faith, and with your leave,' says I, 'I'll not let go the reaping-hook, and the more you bids me, the more I won't let go—so I will.'

" 'You had better, Dan,' says he again.

" 'Why, then, my little fellow,' says I, taking the whole weight of him with my eye from head to foot, 'there are two words to that bargain, and I'll not budge!'

THROUGH FAIRY HALLS

" 'We'll see how that is to be,' says he; and back he went, giving the door such a great bang after him (for it was plain he was huffed) that I thought the moon and all would fall down with it.

"Well, I was preparing myself to try strength with him, when back he comes, with the kitchen cleaver in his hand, and without saying a word he gives two bangs to the handle of the reaping-hook that was holding me up, and *whap*, it came in two. 'Good morning to you, Dan,' says the blackguard, when he saw me cleanly falling down with a bit of the handle in my hand, 'I thank you for your visit, and fair weather after you, Daniel.' I had no time to make any answer to him, for I was tumbling over and over, and rolling and rolling, at the rate of a fox-hunt. 'God help me!' says I. 'But this is a pretty pickle for a decent man to be seen in at this time o' night. I am now sold fairly.' The word was not out of my mouth, when whiz! what should fly by close to my ear but a flock of wild geese, all the way from my own bog of Ballyashenogh, else how should they know *me?* The *ould* gander, who was their general, turning about his head, cried out to me, 'Is that you, Dan?'

" 'The same,' said I.

" 'Good morrow to you,' says he. 'Daniel O'Rourke, how are you in health this morning?'

" 'Very well, sir,' says I, 'thank you kindly!' drawing my breath, for I was mightily in want of some. 'I hope your honour's the same?'

" 'I think 'tis falling you are, Daniel,' says he.

" 'You may say that, sir,' says I.

67

" 'And where are you going so fast?' said the gander, so I told him the whole, terrible story and never the once stopped rolling.

" 'Dan,' says he, 'I'll save you. Put out your hand and catch me by the leg, and I'll fly you home.' Well, I didn't much trust the gander, but there was no help for it. So I caught him by the leg, and away I and the other geese flew as fast as hops.

"We flew, and we flew, and we flew, until we came right over the ocean. 'Ah, my lord,' said I to the goose, for I thought it best to keep a civil tongue in my head, 'fly to land, if you please.'

" 'It is impossible, Dan,' said he, 'we are going to Arabia!'

" 'To Arabia!' said I. 'Oh, Mr. Goose! Why, then, to be sure, I'm a man to be pitied among you.'

" 'Whist, whist, you *impident* rascal,' says he, 'hold your tongue. Arabia is a very decent sort of place.'

"Just as we were talking a ship hove in sight. 'Ah, then, sir,' said I, 'will you drop me on the ship, if you please?'

" 'We are not fair over it,' said he. 'If I dropped you now, you would go splash into the sea.'

" 'I would not,' says I, 'so let me drop at once.'

" 'If you must, you must,' said he. 'There, take your own way'; and he opened his claw, and, faith, he was right—I came down plump into the sea! Down to the very bottom I went and I gave myself up, then, forever, when a whale walked up to me, scratching himself after his night's sleep, and looked me full in the

68

face, and never the word did he say, but, lifting up his tail, he splashed me all over again with the cold salt water till there wasn't a dry stitch on me! And I heard somebody saying— 'twas a voice I knew, too—'Get up, you lazy *vagabond!*' With that I woke up, and there was Judy with a tub full of water, splashing, splashing all over me.

" 'Get up,' says she, 'and to work. Late out o'nights, no reason for *shlapin'* late o' morning. Off with you after the pigs!'

"*Begorra!* of all the places in the parish, there I'd been fast asleep under the *ould* walls of the Pooka's Tower. And what with eagles, and men of the moon, and ganders, and whales, driving me through bogs, and up to the moon, and down to the bottom of the ocean, I never again took forty winks on the road coming home from a party—leastwise not under the Pooka's Tower!"

WILD FLOWERS*

"Of what are you afraid, my child?" inquired the kindly teacher.
"O sir! the flowers, they are *wild*," replied the timid creature.

*From *Pictures and Rhymes*, published by Harper & Brothers.

—*Peter Newell*

HIE AWAY, HIE AWAY
SIR WALTER SCOTT

HIE away, hie away,
Over bank and over brae!
Where the copsewood is the greenest,
Where the fountains glisten sheenest,
Where the lady-fern grows strongest,
Where the morning dew lies longest,
Where the black-cock sweetest sips it,
Where the fairy latest trips it:
Hie to haunts right seldom seen,
Lovely, lonesome, cool, and green!
    Over bank and over brae,
    Hie away, hie away!

The Twelve Months
A Czechoslovakian Fairy Tale

THERE was once a woman who had in her care two children. Katinka, the elder, was the woman's own daughter, and she was as ugly in face as she was in heart, but Dobrunka, the younger, who was only a foster-child, was both beautiful and good. Now the sight of Dobrunka with all her winsome ways, made Katinka appear more than ever hateful and ugly. So the mother and daughter were always in a rage with Dobrunka.

She was made to sweep, cook, wash, sew, spin, weave, cut the grass and take care of the cow, while Katinka lived like a princess. All this Dobrunka did with great good will, but that only made Katinka and her mother the more angry. The better she was, the more plainly did their own wickedness show by contrast, and as they had no wish to do away with their wickedness, they made up their minds to do away with Dobrunka.

One cold day in January, when frost castles glistened on the window panes and the earth was white with snow, Katinka took a fancy for some violets. She called Dobrunka harshly to her and said, "Go to the forest, lazy-bones, and bring me a bunch of violets, that I may put them in my bosom and enjoy their fragrance.

"O sister," answered Dobrunka gently, "I cannot find you any violets under the snow."

But Katinka snapped out angrily, "Hold your tongue and do as I bid you. Go to the forest and bring me back a bunch of violets or you'll find this door forever slammed shut in your face!"

Upon this Katinka and her mother took Dobrunka by the arm, thrust her, without wraps or warm winter clothing, out into the cold, and drew the bolt on her.

71

The poor girl went to the forest weeping sadly. Everything was covered with snow. There was not a foot path anywhere, and the giant pines and oaks bowed their branches low, borne down with their icy burdens. Soon in all this white and glittering wilderness, Dobrunka lost her way and wandered about, famishing with hunger and perishing with cold. Still in her heart she trusted that help would come to one who had done no harm.

All at once she saw a light in the distance, a light that glowed in the sky and quivered now and again as if from the flickering flame of some mighty fire. With her eyes fixed hopefully on that light, Dobrunka climbed toward it. Higher and higher she climbed until at last she reached the top of a giant rock, and there, about a fire, their figures bright in the light and casting long, dark shadows behind, sat twelve motionless figures on twelve great stones. Each figure was wrapped in a long, flowing mantle, his head covered with a hood which fell over his eyes. Three of these mantles were white like the snow, three were green like the grass of the meadows, three were golden like sheaves of ripe wheat, and three were purple as ripened grapes. These twelve figures, who sat there gazing at the fire in perfect silence, were the Beings who governed the Twelve Months of the Year.

Dobrunka knew January by his long, white beard. He was the only one who had a staff in his hand. The sweet girl was confused at this sight, for she was not one to thrust herself forward with strangers. Still she spoke to them with great respect.

"My good sirs, I pray you let me warm myself by your fire; I am freezing with cold."

January nodded his head and motioned her to draw near the blaze.

"Why have you come here, my child?" he asked. "What are you looking for?"

"I am looking for violets," replied Dobrunka.

"This is not the season for violets. Dost thou expect to find violets in the time of snow?" January's voice was gruff.

"Nay," replied Dobrunka sadly, "I know this is not the season for violets, but my foster sister and mother thrust me out of doors and bade me get them. They will never let me come under the shelter of their roof again unless I obey. O my good sirs, can you not tell me where I shall find them?"

Old January rose, and turning to a mere youth in a green mantle, put his staff in his hand and said:

"Brother March, this is your business."

March rose in turn and stirred the fire with the staff, when behold! the flames rose, the snow melted, the buds began to swell on the trees, the grass turned green under the bushes, faint, faint color peeped forth through the green, and the violets opened, —it was Spring.

"Make haste, my child, and gather your violets," said March.

Dobrunka gathered a large bouquet, thanked the Twelve Months, and ran home joyously. Katinka and her mother were struck dumb with astonishment when they saw her spring lightly in with shining face at the doorway. The fragrance of the violets filled the whole house.

"Where did you find these things?" asked Katinka when she had recovered the use of her tongue.

"Up yonder, on the mountain," answered Dobrunka. "It looked like a great blue carpet under the bushes."

But Katinka only snatched away the flowers, put them in her own bosom, and never once said so much as a "Thank you!"

The next morning Katinka, as she sat idling by the stove, took a fancy for some strawberries.

"Go to the forest, good-for-nothing, and bring me some strawberries," cried she to Dobrunka.

"O sister," answered Dobrunka, "but there are no strawberries under the snow."

"Hold your tongue and do as I bid you."

And the mother and daughter took Dobrunka by the arm, thrust her out of the door and drew the bolt on her once again.

So the sweet girl returned to the forest, singing this time to keep up her courage, and looking with all her eyes for the light she had seen the day before. At length she spied it, and reached the great fire, trembling with cold, but still singing.

The Twelve Months were in their places, motionless and silent.

"My good sirs," said Dobrunka, "please to let me warm myself by your fire; I am almost frozen."

"Why have you come hither again?" asked January. "What are you looking for now?"

"I am looking for strawberries," answered she.

"This is not the season for strawberries," growled January, "there are no strawberries under the snow."

"I know it," replied Dobrunka sadly, "but alas! I may never again cross my foster mother's threshold, unless I find them."

Old January rose, and turning to a full grown man in a golden mantle, he put his staff in his hand, saying,

"Brother June, this is your business."

June rose in turn, and stirred the fire with the staff, when behold! the flames rose, the snow melted, the earth grew green, the trees were covered with leaves, the birds sang, the flowers burst into bloom—it was Summer. Thousands of little white stars dotted the green turf, then turned slowly to red strawberries, ripe and luscious in their little green cups.

"Make haste, my child, and gather your strawberries," said June.

Dobrunka filled her apron, thanked the Twelve Months and ran home joyfully. Once again Katinka and her mother were struck dumb with astonishment when they saw her spring lightly in with shining face at the doorway. The fragrance of the strawberries filled the whole house.

"Where did you find these fine things?" asked Katinka, when she had recovered the use of her tongue.

"Up yonder on the mountain," answered Dobrunka as she handed the berries to Katinka, "there were so many of them, that they looked like a crimson carpet on the ground."

Katinka and her mother devoured the strawberries and never once said so much as a "Thank you."

The third day, Katinka took a fancy for some red apples, and she thrust Dobrunka out to fetch them with the same threat she had used before. Dobrunka ran through the snow. So she came once more to the top of the great rock and the motionless figures around the fire.

"You here again, my child?" said January, as he made room for her before the fire. Dobrunka told him sadly it was rosy red apples she must bring home this time.

Old January rose as before.

"Brother September," said he to a man with an iron-gray beard who wore a purple mantle, "this is your business."

September rose and stirred the fire with the staff, when behold! the flames ascended, the snow melted, yellow and crimson leaves appeared on the trees, gently a brown leaf floated down—it was autumn. But Dobrunka saw one thing only, an apple tree with its rosy fruit.

"Make haste, my child, shake the tree," said September.

Dobrunka shook it; an apple fell; she shook it again, and down fell another.

"Now take what thou hast and hurry home!" cried September.

So the sweet girl thanked the Twelve Months and obediently ran back home. Now the astonishment of Katinka and her mother knew no bounds—

"Apples in January! Where did you get them?" asked Katinka.

"Up yonder on the mountain; there is a tree there loaded down with them."

"Why did you bring only these two? You ate the rest on the way!"

"Nay, sister, I did not touch them. I was only permitted to shake the tree twice, so only two apples fell down."

At that Katinka cried angrily, "I do not believe you. You have eaten the rest. Begone!" and she drove Dobrunka out

76

of the room. Then she sat down and ate one of the apples while her mother ate the other. Their flavor was delicious. They had never tasted the like before.

"Mother," cried Katinka, "Give me my warm fur cloak. I must have more of these apples. I shall go to the mountain, find the tree and shake it as long as I like, whether I am permitted or not. I shall bring back for myself all the delicious fruit on the tree."

The mother tried to stop her from going forth into the wintry forest. But the spoiled daughter would not heed her. Wrapping herself in her warm fur coat, and pulling the hood down over her ears, she hurried away.

Everything was covered with snow, there was not even a foot path. Katinka lost her way, but, urged on by greedy desire

for the apples, she still went forward till she spied a light in the distance. Then she climbed and she climbed till at last she reached the place where the Twelve Months sat about their fire. But she knew not who they were, so she pushed rudely through their midst and up to the fire without even a "By your leave."

"Why have you come here? What do you want?" asked old January gruffly.

"What matters it to you, old man?" answered Katinka. "It is none of your business." And without another word she turned and disappeared in the forest.

January frowned till his brow was black as a storm cloud. He raised his staff above his head, and in a twinkling, the fire went out, black darkness covered the earth, the wind rose and the snow fell.

Katinka could not see the way before her. The snow beat on her face and into her eyes and loomed up, mountains high, before her. She lost herself and vainly tried to find the way home. She called her mother, she cursed her sister, she shrieked out wildly. The snow fell and the wind blew, the snow fell and the wind blew—

The mother looked for her darling ceaselessly. First from the door and then from the window, and then from the door and then from the window. The hours passed—the clock struck midnight and still Katinka did not return.

"I shall go and look for my daughter," said the mother. So she wrapped herself warmly in her great fur cloak and hood and waded off through the drifts into the forest.

Everything was covered with snow; there was not even a foot path. At each step the woman called out through the storm for her daughter. The snow fell and the wind blew, the snow fell and the wind blew—

THROUGH FAIRY HALLS

Dobrunka waited at home through the night but no one returned. In the morning she sat herself down at her spinning wheel and began to spin, but ever and again she sprang up and looked out at the window.

"What can have happened?" she said. But the only answer was the glare of the sun on the ice and the cracking of the branches beneath their heavy burdens.

Winter passed and summer came, but Katinka and her mother never returned to the little cottage beside the forest. So the house, the cow, the garden and the meadow fell to Dobrunka. In the course of time her Prince came. She married and the place resounded with laughter and joy and singing. The Spring Months called the world into bloom for her; Summer brought her flowers and sunny skies and green things growing; Autumn filled her storehouses with golden grain and ripened fruit, and Winter gave her sweet home joys with her little ones by the blazing hearth. No matter how much the North wind blew, and the house shook, and the snow fell—there was always spring and summer in Dobrunka's heart. So the roses climbed up over her cottage, the sweetest song birds sang at her door, her blossoming fruit trees perfumed the air, and the laughter of her children made music everywhere.

PROVIDENCE

When all thy mercies, O my God,
  My rising soul surveys,
Transported with the view, I'm lost
  In wonder, love, and praise.

Ten thousand thousand precious gifts
  My daily thanks employ;
Nor is the least a cheerful heart,
  That tastes those gifts with joy.
                    —*Joseph Addison.*

79

The Princess on the Glass Hill*

SIR GEORGE WEBBE DASENT

ONCE on a time there was a man who had a meadow, which lay high up on the hillside, and in the meadow was a barn, which he had built to keep his hay in. Now, I must tell you there hadn't been much in the barn for the last year or two, for every St. John's night, when the grass stood greenest and deepest, the meadow was eaten down to the very ground just as if a whole drove of sheep had been there feeding on it over night. This happened once, it happened twice; so at last the man grew weary of losing his crop of hay, and said to his sons—for he had three of them, and the youngest was nicknamed Boots, of course—that now one of them must go and sleep in the barn in the outlying field when St. John's night came, for it was too good a joke that his grass should be eaten, root and blade, this year, as it had been the last two years. So whichever of them went must keep a sharp lookout; that was what their father said.

Well, the eldest son was ready to go and watch the meadow; trust him for looking after the grass! It shouldn't be his fault if man or beast got a blade of grass. So, when evening came, he set off to the barn, and lay down to sleep; but a little on in the night came such a clatter, and such an earthquake, that walls and roof shook, and groaned, and creaked; then up jumped the lad, and took to his heels as fast as ever he could; nor dared he once look round till he reached home; and as for the hay, why it was eaten up this year just as it had been twice before.

The next St. John's night, the man said again it would never do to lose all the grass in the outlying field year after year in this

*From *Popular Tales from the Norse*, published by G. P. Putnam's Sons.

way, so one of his sons must just trudge off to watch it, and
watch it well, too. Well, the next oldest son was ready to try
his luck, so he set off, and lay down to sleep in the barn as his
brother had done before him; but as night wore on there came on
a rumbling and quaking of the earth, worse even than on the
last St. John's night, and when the lad heard it he got frightened,
and took to his heels as though he were running a race.

Next year the turn came to Boots; but when he made ready to
go, the other two began to laugh, and to make game of him, saying,—

"You're just the man to watch the hay, that you are; you
who have done nothing all your life but sit in the ashes and toast
yourself by the fire."

But Boots did not care a pin for their chattering, and stumped
away, as evening drew on, up the hill-side to the outlying field.
There he went inside the barn and lay down; but in about an
hour's time the barn began to groan and creak, so that it was
dreadful to hear.

"Well," said Boots to himself, "if it isn't worse than this, I
can stand it well enough."

A little while after came another creak and an earthquake,
so that the litter in the barn flew about the lad's ears.

"Oh!" said Boots to himself, "if it isn't worse than this, I daresay I can stand it out."

But just then came a third rumbling, and a third earthquake, so that the lad thought walls and roof were coming down on his head; but it passed off, and all was still as death about him.

"It'll come again, I'll be bound," thought Boots; but no, it did not come again; still it was and still it stayed; but after he had lain a little while he heard a noise as if a horse were standing just outside the barn-door. He peeped through a chink, and there stood a horse feeding away. So big, and fat, and grand a horse, Boots had never set eyes on; by his side on the grass lay a saddle and bridle, and a full set of armour for a knight, all of brass, so bright that the light gleamed from it.

"Ho, ho!" thought the lad; "it's you, is it, that eats up our hay? I'll soon put a spoke in your wheel; just see if I don't."

So he lost no time, but took the steel out of his tinder-box, and threw it over the horse; then it had no power to stir from the spot, and became so tame that the lad could do what he liked with it. So he got on its back, and rode off with it to a place which no one knew of, and there he put up the horse. When he got home his brothers laughed, and asked how he had fared?

"You didn't lie long in the barn, even if you had the heart to go as far as the field."

"Well," said Boots, "all I can say is, I lay in the barn till the sun rose, and neither saw nor heard anything; I can't think what there was in the barn to make you both so afraid."

"A pretty story!" said his brothers. "But we'll soon see how you have watched the meadow." So they set off; but when they reached it, there stood the grass as deep and thick as it had been over night.

Well, the next St. John's eve it was the same story over again; neither of the older brothers dared to go out to the outlying field to watch the crop; but Boots, he had the heart to go, and everything happened just as it had happened the year before. First a clatter and an earthquake, then a greater clatter and another earthquake, and so on a third time; only this year the earthquakes were far worse than the year before. Then all at once everything was as still as death and the lad heard how something was cropping the grass outside the barn-door, so he stole to the door, and peeped through a chink; and what do you think he saw? Why, another horse standing right up against the wall, and chewing and champing with might and main. It was far finer and fatter than that which came the year before, and it had a saddle on its back and a bridle on its neck, and a full suit of mail for a knight lay by its side, all of silver, and as grand as you would wish to see.

"Ho, ho!" said Boots to himself; "it's you that gobbles up our hay, is it? I'll soon put a spoke in your wheel;" and with that he took the steel out of his tinder-box, and threw it over the horse's crest, which stood as still as a lamb. Well, the lad rode this horse, too, to the hiding-place where he kept the other one, and after that he went home.

"I suppose you'll tell us," said one of his brothers, "there's a fine crop this year, too, up in the hayfield."

"Well, so there is," said Boots; and off ran the others to see. There stood the grass and thick and deep, as it was the year before; but they didn't give Boots softer words for all that.

Now, when the third St. John's eve came, the two elder still hadn't the heart to lie out in the barn and watch the grass, for they had got so scared at heart the night they lay there before, but Boots, he dared to go; and, to make a long story short, the very same thing happened this time as had happened twice before. Three earthquakes came, one after the other each worse than the one which went before, and when the last came, the

lad danced about with the shock from one barn wall to the other;
and, after that, all at once, it was still as death. Now when he
had lain a little while he heard something tugging away at the
grass outside the barn, so he stole again to the door-chink, and
peeped out, and there stood a horse close outside—far, far bigger
and fatter than the two he had taken before.

"Ho, ho!" said the lad to himself, "it's you, is it, that comes
here eating up our hay? I'll soon stop that—I'll soon put a
spoke in your wheel." So he caught up his steel and threw it
over the horse's neck, and in a trice it stood as if it were nailed
to the ground, and Boots could do as he pleased with it. Then
he rode off with it to the hiding-place where he kept the other
two, and then went home. When he got home his two brothers
made game of him as they had done before, saying they could
see he had watched the grass well, for he looked for all the world
as if he were walking in his sleep, and many other spiteful things
they said, but Boots gave no heed to them, only asking them to

go and see for themselves; and when they went, there stood the grass as fine and deep this time as it had been twice before.

Now, you must know that the King of the country where Boots lived had a daughter, whom he would only give to the man who could ride up over the hill of glass, for there was a high, high, high hill, all of glass, as smooth and slippery as ice, close to the King's palace. Upon the tip-top of the hill the King's daughter was to sit, with three golden apples in her lap, and the man who could ride up and carry off the three golden apples was to have half the kingdom, and the Princess to wife. This the King had stuck up on all the church-doors in his realm, and had given it out in many other kingdoms besides. Now, this Princess was so lovely that all who set eyes on her fell over head and ears in love with her whether they would or no. So I needn't tell you how all the princes and knights who heard of her were eager to win her and half the kingdom beside; and how they came riding from all parts of the world on high prancing horses, and clad in the grandest clothes, for there wasn't one of them who hadn't made up his mind that he, and he alone, was to win the Princess.

So when the day of trial came, which the King had fixed, there was such a crowd of princes and knights under the glass hill that it made one's head whirl to look at them; and every one in the country who could even crawl along was off to the hill, for they were eager to see the man who was to win the Princess. So the two elder brothers set off with the rest; but as for Boots, they said outright he shouldn't go with them, for if they were seen with such a dirty lad, all begrimed with smut from cleaning their shoes and sifting cinders in the dusthole, they said folk would make game of them.

"Very well," said Boots, "it's all one to me. I can go alone, and stand or fall by myself."

Now when the two brothers came to the hill of glass the knights and princes were all hard at it, riding their horses till they were all in a foam; but it was no good, by my troth; for as soon as ever the horses set foot on the hill, down they slipped, and there wasn't one who could get a yard or two up; and no wonder, for the hill was as smooth as a sheet of glass, and as steep as a house-wall. But all were eager to have the Princess and half the kingdom. So they rode and slipped, and slipped and rode, and still it was the same story over again. At last all their horses were so weary that they could scarce lift a leg, and in such a sweat that the lather dripped from them, and so the knights had to give up trying any more. So the King was just thinking that he would proclaim a new trial for the next day, to see if they would have better luck, when all at once a knight came riding up on so brave a steed no one had ever seen the like of it in his born days, and the knight had mail of brass, and the horse a brass bit in his mouth, so bright that the sunbeams shone from it. Then all the others called out to him he might just as well spare himself the trouble of riding at the hill, for it would lead to no good; but he gave no heed to them, and put his horse at the hill, and went up it like nothing for a good way, about a third of the height; and when he got so far, he turned his horse round and rode down again. So lovely a knight the Princess thought she had never yet seen, and while he was riding she sat and thought to herself—

"Would to heaven he might only come up, and down the other side."

And when she saw him turning back, she threw down one of the golden apples after him, and it rolled down into his shoe. But when he got to the bottom of the hill he rode off so fast that no one could tell what had become of him. That evening all the knights and princes were to go before the King that he who

86

had ridden so far up the hill might show the apple which the Princess had thrown, but there was no one who had anything to show. One after the other they all came, but not a man could show the apple.

At even the brothers of Boots came home, too, and had such a long story to tell about the riding up the hill.

"First of all," they said, "there was not one of the whole lot who could get so much as a stride up; but at last came one who had a suit of brass mail, and a brass bridle and saddle, all so bright that the sun shone from them a mile off. He was a chap to ride, just! He rode a third of the way up the hill of glass, and he could easily have ridden the whole way up, if he chose; but he turned round and rode down, thinking, maybe, that was enough for once."

"Oh! I should so like to have seen him, that I should," said Boots, who sat by the fireside, and stuck his feet into the cinders as was his wont.

"Oh!" said his brothers, "you would, would you? You look fit to keep company with such high lords, dirty fellow that you are sitting there amongst the ashes."

Next day the brothers were all for setting off again, and Boots begged them this time, too, to let him go with them and see the riding but, no, they wouldn't have him at any price.

"Well, well!" said Boots; "if I go at all, I must go by myself. I'm not afraid."

So when the brothers got to the hill of glass, all the princes and knights began to ride again, and you may fancy they had taken care to shoe their horses sharp; but it was no good—they rode and slipped, and slipped and rode, just as they had done the day before, and there was not one who could get so far as a yard up the hill. And when they had worn out their horses, so that they could not stir a leg, they were all forced to give it up as a bad job. So the King thought he might as well proclaim that the riding should take place the day after for the last time, just to give them one chance more; but all at once it came across his mind that he might as well wait a little longer, to see if the knight in brass mail would come this day too. Well, they saw nothing of him, but all at once came one riding on a steed far, far braver and finer than that on which the knight in brass had ridden, and he had silver mail, and a silver saddle all so bright that the sunbeams gleamed and glanced from them far away. Then the others shouted out to him again, saying he might as well hold hard, and not try to ride up the hill, for all his trouble would be thrown away; but the knight paid no heed to them, and rode straight at the hill, and right up it, till he had gone two-thirds of the way, and then he wheeled his horse round and rode down again. To tell the truth, the Princess liked him still better than the knight in brass, and she sat and wished he might only be able to come right up to the top and down the other side; but when she saw him turning back she threw the second apple after him, and it rolled down and fell into his shoe. But as soon as ever he had come down from the hill of glass, he rode off so fast that no one could see what became of him.

At even, when all were to go in before the King and the Princess, that he who had the golden apple might show it, in they went, one after the other, but there was no one who had any apple to show, and the two brothers, as they had done on the former day, went home and told how things had gone, and how all had ridden at the hill and none got up.

"But, last of all," they said, "came one in a silver suit, and his horse had a silver saddle and a silver bridle. He was just a chap to ride; and he got two-thirds up the hill, and then turned back. He was a fine fellow and no mistake; and the Princess threw the second gold apple to him."

89

"Oh!" said Boots, "I should so like to have seen him, too, that I should."

"A pretty story!" they said. "Perhaps you think his coat of mail was as bright as the ashes you are always poking about!"

The third day everything happened as it had happened the two days before. There was no one who could get so much as a yard up the hill; and now all waited for the knight in silver mail, but they neither saw nor heard of him. At last came one riding on a steed, so brave that no one had ever seen his match; and the knight had a suit of golden mail, and a golden saddle and bridle, so wondrous bright that the sunbeams gleamed from them a mile off. The other knights and princes could not find time to call out to him not to try his luck, for they were amazed to see how grand he was. So he rode at the hill, and tore up it like nothing, so that the Princess hadn't even time to wish that he might get up the whole way. As soon as ever he reached the top, he took the third golden apple from the Princess' lap, and then turned his horse and rode down again. As soon as he got down, he rode off at full speed, and was out of sight in no time.

Now, when the brothers got home at even, you may fancy what long stories they told, how the riding had gone off that day; and amongst other things, they had a deal to say about the knight in golden mail.

"He just was a chap to ride!" they said, "so grand a knight isn't to be found in the wide world."

"Oh!" said Boots, "I should so like to have seen him; that I should."

Next day all the knights and princes were to pass before the King and the Princess—it was too late to do so the night before, I suppose—that he who had the gold apple might bring it forth; but one came after another, first the princes, and then the knights, and still there was no one who could show the gold apple.

"Well," said the King, "some one must have it, for it was something that we all saw with our own eyes, how a man came and rode up and bore it off."

So he commanded that every one who was in the kingdom should come up to the palace and see if they could show the apple. Well, they all came, one after another, but no one had the golden apple, and after a long time the two brothers of Boots came. They were the last of all, so the King asked them if there was no one else in the kingdom who hadn't come.

"Oh, yes," said they, "we have a brother, but he never carried off the golden apple. He hasn't stirred out of the dust-hole on any of the three days."

"Never mind that," said the King; "he may as well come up to the palace like the rest."

So Boots had to go up to the palace.

"How, now," said the King; "have you got the golden apple? Speak out!"

"Yes, I have," said Boots; "here is the first, and here is the second, and there is the third, too;" and with that he pulled all three golden apples out of his pocket, and at the same time threw off his sooty rags, and stood before them in his gleaming golden mail.

"Yes!" said the King; "you shall have my daughter and half my kingdom, for you well deserve both her and it."

So they got ready for the wedding, and Boots got the Princess to wife, and there was great merry-making at the bridal-feast, you may fancy, for they could all be merry though they couldn't ride up the hill of glass; and all I can say is, if they haven't left off their merry-making yet, why, they're still at it.

The Three Wishes
A Spanish Fairy Tale

One winter's night many years ago, an old man, named Pedro, and his wife, Joanna, sat by their cozy fire, talking to one another, in a little old village in Spain. Now Pedro was comfortably well off in the goods of this world, but instead of giving thanks to God for the benefits they enjoyed, he and his wife spent all their time in wishing for the good things possessed by their neighbors.

"Bah!" cried Pedro. "This wretched little hut of ours is only fit to house a donkey! I wish we had the fine house and farm of our neighbor, Diego!"

"Aye! Diego's house and farm are well enough," answered Joanna. "Still I should like a mansion such as the grandees possess—such a one as that of Don Juan de la Rosa."

"Then there's that old donkey of ours," went on Pedro sullenly. "Good for nothing—nothing at all. He cannot carry an empty sack! Would that I owned Diego's strong Andalusian mule!"

"O aye!" said Joanna. "Diego's mule is better than our donkey. Yet, for me, I should like a white horse with trappings of scarlet and gold, like Donna Isabella's. Strange how some people have only to wish in order to get a thing. I've never been in such luck. Would that we had but to speak to have our wishes come true!"

Scarcely were the words out of Joanna's mouth when lo! on the hearth before the old couple appeared a beautiful little lady. She was not more than eighteen inches high and her garments were white and filmy and full of opal tints as though made of smoke, while a smoky veil floated down from a crown of sparks on her head. In her hand she bore a little golden wand, on the end of which glowed a single spark.

"I am the Fairy Fortunata," said she. "I have heard your complaints and am come to give you what you desire. Three

wishes you shall have,—one for you, Joanna,—one for you, Pedro,
—and the third you shall agree upon between you, and I will
grant it in person when I return at this time tomorrow."

So saying, the Fairy Fortunata sprang through the flames and
disappeared. Ah! but the old couple were delighted. Three
wishes to come true! They began to think at once of what they
most desired in all the world. Wishes came swarming to them as
thick as bees to a hive. The old man would be content with such
prosperity as his neighbor, the farmer Diego, enjoyed, but the old
woman—ah! her desires flew high—a palace with domes and spires
and cupolas, and floors tiled with sapphire, and walls and ceilings
done with arabesques of crimson, blue and gold; colonnaded
courtyards with fountains playing in the centre, and gardens and
servants and what not besides! Well, so many were the desires
that came crowding to the old couple, that they could not agree
off-hand on just which three to wish for. So they determined to

put off their decision until the next day and began talking of different things altogether.

"I dropped in at Diego's this morning," said Pedro, "and they were making black puddings. Um! but they smelled good! Diego can buy the best of food. He does not have to put up with such poor stuff as we have to eat!"

"True! True!" said Joanna. "I wish I had one of Diego's puddings this minute to roast on the ashes for supper!"

The words were not out of Joanna's mouth when presto! on the hearth appeared a delicious black pudding! The woman's eyes opened wide; but Pedro jumped up in a rage.

"You greedy creature!" he cried. "You have used up one of our precious wishes! Good heavens, to wish for nothing more than one poor little pudding! It makes me wild, you goose! I wish the silly pudding were stuck fast to your nose!"

Whisk! Flop! Splotch! there flew the great black pudding and hung from Joanna's nose. The old man shrieked in surprise. Joanna gurgled with horror; but shake her head as she might, she could no more shake off the pudding than she could shake off her nose!

"See what you have done, you evil tongue!" she wailed. "If I employed my wish badly, it injured only myself, but you—you—look!"

Thereupon, the dog and cat, having sniffed the savory pudding, came leaping up, springing and pawing, to lick that luscious morsel that was now Dame Joanna's nose!

"Down! Down!" shrieked Joanna, as she wildly defended the part attacked. "I shall agree to nothing else for our third wish than that this miserable pudding be taken off my nose!"

"Wife, for heaven's sake!" cried Pedro, "don't ask that! What of the new farm I wanted?"

"I will never agree to wish for it!"

"But listen to reason! Think of the palace you desired, with domes and spires and cupolas, and walls of crimson and gold."

"It does not matter!"

"O my dear! let us wish at least for a fortune, and then you shall have a golden case set with all the jewels you please, to cover the pudding on your nose!"

"I will not hear of it!"

"Then, alas and alack, we shall be left just as we were before!"

"That is all I desire! I see now we were well enough off as we were!"

And for all the man could say, nothing could change his wife's mind. And so at last they agreed. On the following night the Fairy rose from the flames and bade them tell her their third wish, but they answered both together:

"We wish only to be as we were before."

And lo, their wish was granted.

MY BOOK HOUSE

A BOY'S SONG

JAMES HOGG

WHERE the pools are bright and deep,
  Where the gray trout lies asleep,
Up the river and o'er the lea,
That's the way for Billy and me.

Where the blackbird sings the latest,
Where the hawthorn blooms the sweetest,
Where the nestlings chirp and flee,
That's the way for Billy and me.

Where the mowers mow the cleanest,
Where the hay lies thick and greenest,—
There to trace the homeward bee,
That's the way for Billy and me.

Where the hazel bank is steepest,
Where the shadow lies the deepest,
Where the clustering nuts fall free,
That's the way for Billy and me.

APRIL*
JOHN GALSWORTHY

STARRY-EYED in April morn,
Rain bells glitter on the thorn.
Birds are tuning down the lane
Patter song of fallen rain.
Spring can grieve, but Spring can be
Very life of minstrelsy!

Gorse has lit his lanterns all,
Cob-webbed thrift's a fairy ball,
Earth it smells as good as new,
Winds are merry, sky is blue.

*From *Moods, Songs and Doggerels*. Reprinted by permission of the publishers, Charles Scribner's Sons.

The Squire's Bride
PETER CHRISTEN ASBJÖRNSEN

NCE upon a time there was a rich squire who owned a large farm and had plenty of silver at the bottom of his chest and money in the bank besides; but he felt there was something wanting, for he was a widower.

One day the daughter of a neighboring farmer was working for him in the hay field. The squire saw her and liked her very much, and as she was the child of poor parents, he thought if he only hinted that he wanted her she would be ready to marry him at once. So he told her he had been thinking of getting married again.

"Ay! one may think of many things," said the girl, laughing. In her opinion the old fellow ought to be thinking of something that behooved him better than getting married.

"Well, you see, I thought that you should be my wife!"

"No, thank you all the same," said she, "that's not at all likely."

The squire was not accustomed to be gainsaid, and the more she refused him, the more determined he was to get her. But as he made no progress in her favor, he sent for her father and told him that if he could arrange the matter with his daughter he would forgive him the money he had lent him, and he would also give him the piece of land which lay close to his meadow into the bargain.

"Yes, you may be sure I'll bring my daughter to her senses," said the father. "She is only a child and she doesn't know what's best for her." But all his coaxing and talking did not help matters. She would not have the squire, she said, if he sat buried in gold up to his ears.

The squire waited day after day, but at last he became so angry and impatient that he told the father, if he expected him to stand by his promise, he would have to put his foot down and settle the matter now, for he would not wait any longer.

THROUGH FAIRY HALLS

The man knew no other way out of it but to let the squire get everything ready for the wedding; and when the parson and wedding guests had arrived, the squire should send for the girl as if she was wanted for some work on the farm. When she arrived she would have to be married right away, so that she would have no time to think it over. The squire thought this was well and good, and so he began brewing and baking and getting ready for the wedding in grand style. When the guests had arrived, the squire called one of his farm lads and told him to run down to his neighbor and ask him to send him what he had promised.

"But if you are not back in a twinkling," he said, shaking his fist at him, "I'll—"

He did not say more, for the lad ran off as if he had been shot at.

"My master has sent me to ask for what you promised him," said the lad when he got to the neighbor, "but there is no time to be lost for he is terribly busy today."

"Yes, yes! Run down into the meadow and take her with you. There she goes!" answered the neighbor.

The lad ran off and when he came to the meadow he found the daughter there raking hay.

"I am to fetch what your father has promised my master," said the lad.

"Ah, ha!" thought she. "Is that what they are up to?"

"Ah, indeed," she said, "I suppose it's that little bay mare of ours. You had better go and take her. She stands there tethered on the other side of the peas field," said the girl.

The boy jumped on the back of the bay mare and rode home at full gallop.

"Have you got her with you?" asked the squire.

"She is down at the door," said the lad.

"Take her up to the room my mother had," said the squire.

"But master, how can that be managed?" said the lad.

"You must just do as I tell you," said the squire. "If you cannot manage her alone you must get the men to help you," for he thought the girl might turn obstreperous.

When the lad saw his master's face he knew it would be no use to gainsay him. So he went and got all the farm tenants who were there to help him. Some pulled at the head and the forelegs of the mare and others pushed from behind, and at last they got her up the stairs and into the room. There lay all the wedding finery ready.

"Now that's done, master!" said the lad; "but it was a terrible job. It was the worst I have ever had here on the farm."

"Never mind, you shall not have done it for nothing," said his master. "Now send the women up to dress her."

"But I say, master—!" said the lad.

"None of your talk!" said the squire. "Tell them they must dress her and mind and not forget either wreath or crown."

The lad ran into the kitchen.

"Look here, lasses," he said, "you must go upstairs and dress up the bay mare as bride. I expect the master wants to give the guests a laugh!"

The women dressed the bay mare in everything that was there, and then the lad went and told his master that now she was ready dressed, with wreath and crown and all.

"Very well, bring her down!" said the squire. "I will receive her myself at the door."

There was a terrible clatter on the stairs; for that bride, you know, had no silken shoes on. When the door was opened and the squire's bride entered the parlor you can imagine there was a good deal of tittering and grinning.

And as for the squire you may be sure he had had enough of that bride, and they say he never went courting again.

How Yehl, the Hero, Freed
the Beaming Maiden

An Alaskan Legend

ALL Alaska was once in a dim, gray twilight. There was neither sun, moon, nor stars in the sky. In those days there lived in Alaska a proud and powerful chief, named Chet'l. On the totem pole before his lodge was carved the figure of the raven, on his deerhorn spoons was carved the raven, into his blankets was woven the raven, on his canoes was painted the raven. For Chet'l belonged to the Raven clan.

"Raven keeps guard over Chet'l!" the Chief often boasted. But he was dark and stormy by nature, easily roused to violent rages and his sister, Nuschagak, who lived with him, suffered much from the roaring tempests of his fury.

"Raven keeps guard over quiet one!" she would cry. "Not over stormy one like you! One who always shrieks, 'I! I! I!'"

So Chet'l would have none of Nuschagak in his lodge, he drove her out to live by herself, and there dwelt with him no woman.

Then one dim, gray day he rose up and went far, far into the Northland. There in the midst of the ice and snow, he saw a maiden of dazzling beauty, more beautiful than anything man had ever beheld before. When she smiled her face beamed and light streamed forth on all about.

"Maiden go back with Chet'l to his lodge!" cried the Chief. So the Maiden gave him her hand and glided along by his side. When they were come to his home, Chet'l gave her rich furs to lie on and many precious blankets. He never asked her to make the fire or do the work of woman. But, though he loaded her with gifts, he wished to keep her all to himself.

"Keep your smiles alone for Chet'l!" he cried.

"Nay," replied the maiden, "I was not made to make happy one only. I smile on all alike. I give my love to all."

Then was Chet'l as the storm cloud.

"Smile on any other," he roared, "and Chet'l buries you deep, where none shall have joy of your beaming!"

"Ah," the maiden made answer, "bury me as deep as you like. You will only shut yourself out from my smile. You can never quench my beaming. I shall go on smiling forever."

Then went Chet'l and fetched eight small redbirds. He whispered to them, "Stand guard over this rebellious maid while Chet'l goes out hunting. See that she smiles on no one. Thus bids thee the great Chet'l." And he fastened the door of his lodge from without and strode away into the forest.

No sooner was he gone than the maiden rose and went to the door. Lo! as she beamed on the solid wood, a little opening appeared; she leaned her head through the opening and smiled on all who passed. And all on whom she smiled felt warmed and cheered and strengthened.

"We bloom as the young grass," they cried, "as the grass when the snow is gone."

Then the little redbirds made great noise and clamor. Out they flew by the hole in the roof, through which the smoke escaped from the hearth—off and away to tell Chet'l.

Thundering with anger, his eyes flashing lightnings, back came Chet'l. He seized the beautiful maiden and thrust her into a great wooden chest. Then he forced down the lid, made fast the lock, and carried the chest away to a dark little inner room that no one was ever permitted to enter.

"There," said he, "now that smile is hid where Chet'l shares it with no man."

Ah, but the world was dark, and in it was no joy at all for Chet'l. All the people began to wail and lament. Never before was such darkness.

"Give her back to us, the Maiden-that-beams!" they cried, yet Chet'l would not relent and restore to them the maiden.

Then came to Chet'l Nuschagak, his sister.

"Set her free—the Maiden," said Nuschagak. "On your totem pole the raven frowns—frowns at the deed that Chet'l has done."

Up rose Chet'l like a whirlwind! He fell on his sister's lodge and hacked it to pieces. And he hacked to pieces also the totem pole before her door, casting the raven to the wind.

"Chet'l cares not for the raven," he cried. "Chet'l does as he pleases. And you, little snarling fox, forth with you into the forests, and come no more back to Chet'l, lest he serve you as he did the maiden."

In grief and sorrow, Nuschagak wandered down to the sea. As she stood there, weeping, lo! a raven appeared before her.

"Be not sad, good daughter," said the Raven. "You shall have a child that will be greater than Chet'l. Train him up to be a man and he will yet save you and the Maid."

So Nuschagak went away, built a rude lodge in the forest and set up before it the totem pole of the raven. Soon there came to her a son. The child was beautiful and wonderful. In ten days he had grown to the height of a man and mastered all the knowledge that belongs to manhood. Then the mother knew that there had come to her Yehl, the hero. Yehl, the Great One, greater than Chet'l!

Yehl, who could save both her and the Maid and with them all the people!

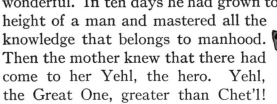
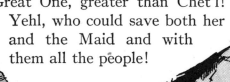

THROUGH FAIRY HALLS

When Yehl had made Nuschagak a comfortable lodge and gathered for her a goodly store of food, she sent him forth to face Chet'l. Straight to the great chief's lodge went Yehl.

"I am your sister's son," said he. Then Chet'l saw that he was a goodly youth and dared not do less than bid him welcome, but in his heart he said, "He knows the secret of the Maid. I shall soon find means to be rid of him."

When there came the dim gray dawn that was all there was to the next day's light, he took Yehl in his canoe and paddled out to sea—"to fish for great fish," said Chet'l. Far, far out he went till the shore had long faded from sight, and the waters lay black, of boundless depth, beneath their rocking keel. Then Chet'l overturned the canoe and plunged Yehl into the deep.

"Let him find a lodge with the whales," cried he. "He is not welcome to Chet'l!" and he righted his canoe and made his way back to shore.

But Yehl dropped quietly to the bottom of the sea, walked safely over the smooth, hard sand and appeared at evening in the door of his uncle's lodge!

"Hah!" muttered Chet'l. "Some whale must have borne him back to shore. Mayhap the whale is his totem! But there be other means to put him out of my way."

The next day he took Yehl out into the forest. There, set up high on poles in the midst of a deep dark grove of cypress, spruce and hemlock, was a great canoe that Chet'l had been building. It was hewn of a solid log, and had been burned with fire to hollow out the center.

"Step into the canoe, Son-of-my-sister," said Chet'l, "and chip off the burnt wood about the sides to make the inside smooth."

Yehl did as his uncle bade him, but while he was bent over at work, Chet'l sent a great log crashing down and pinned him in where he sat.

105

"If whale be your totem," he jeered, "what can save you now?"

No sooner was he gone, than Yehl stretched out his arms. At that, the canoe fell to pieces and Yehl stepped forth from under the log. Then he picked up the different parts of the craft, put them together again, and finished it, complete. That evening he appeared at the door of Chet'l's lodge bearing the great canoe on his shoulder.

Then Chet'l's tongue was dumb. But when the night was come, he crept up to the couch of skins whereon his nephew slumbered. "I shall have you yet!" cried he. Just as his hand was at the youth's throat, Yehl turned himself into a raven, slipped out of his grasp and flew up into the sky.

"Ah, he is the Raven, the Raven himself!" cried Chet'l, and he minded how he had cried out that he cared not for the Raven, but would do what pleased himself. "No use to contend with the Raven!" And he plunged off into the forest.

Then came Yehl back to the lodge and found his way to the

darkened chamber. He groped about in the gloom till he came upon a chest.

"Now," said he, "at last I shall set free the Maid." Up came the lid beneath his grasp, but out of the chest rose no Maid. Instead, there flew forth a glistening flock of tiny white birds that darted up into the sky and lo! they became the stars.

Then Yehl groped about again till he once more fell upon something. He pulled up the lid of a second chest. But still no maiden appeared. One great silver bird with pale, gleaming wings soared up into the sky and lo! it became the moon.

"Yehl will not rest till he finds her!" cried the youth, and he searched again till he found a third and last chest. Heavy was its lid—far heavier than the others. He forced it up but a little way and a light shone forth through the crack, like the first faint rose of dawn. As he pulled it higher and higher, the light became dazzling gold, streamed forth in boundless splendor and flooded all the room. Then up rose the smiling Maiden.

"Well done, Yehl," said she. And she floated in shimmering glory up to the sky. Behold! She was the Sun.

Then Yehl rejoiced and Nuschagak rejoiced and all the people on earth rejoiced.

"It is gone—the cold and dark!" they cried. "Light and warmth are come! Behold we bloom again like grass when the snow is melted!"

As to Chet'l, when he found that Yehl had loosed the shining Maid to shine forever on all the world, he went off and hid himself in a dark cave on Mt. Edgecomb. There he became the Thunderbird. He is still trying to shut up the Sun and keep her from beaming. When he comes forth, the flapping of his great wings makes the thunder and the flash of his eyes the lightning, but no matter what walls of clouds he builds up, the Sun always finds a way through them. Thanks to Yehl, she is still in the sky, beaming with gentle radiance on everyone alike.

The Luck Boy of Toy Valley*

Katherine Dunlap Cather

IN A chalet high up among the Austrian mountains, blue-eyed Franz was very unhappy because his mother and brother Johan were going to Vienna, and he had to stay at home with his old grandfather. He bit his lips to keep back the tears as he watched the packing of the box that was to carry their clothing. Then his mother tried to comfort him.

"Never mind, lad," she said. "I'll send you a present from Vienna, and we'll call it a 'luck gift' and hope it will bring good luck. If it does, you'll be a lucky boy."

He smiled even if he did feel sad. He had often heard of luck children, for, among the Tyrolean peasants, there were many stories of those who had been led by fairies to have such wonderful good fortune that ever afterward they were spoken of as the elf-aided, or "Glücks Kinder," and it was so delightful to think about being one of them that he forgot his sorrow. Of course it would be very fine to travel down to Vienna and go into the service of a rich noble there, as his mother and brother were to do, but it would be still better to be a "Glücks Kind," and such things sometimes did happen. So he did not feel sad any more, but whistled and sang and helped with the packing. Early next morning the post chaise rattled up to the door, and Johan

*Used by the courteous permission of David C. Cook Publishing Co. and the author.

and the mother drove away. Franz watched them go down the winding, white road, calling after them in sweet Tyrolean words of endearment until they were out of sight. Then he went back into the hut and began to sandpaper some blocks that his grandfather needed for his work. The old man was a maker of picture frames, all carved and decorated with likenesses of mountain flowers; and these, when sent to Innobruck and Vienna, brought the money that gave him his living. The figures were too fine and difficult for Franz to carve, but he could lend a hand at fetching blocks and sandpapering. He worked with a vim, for Tyrolean boys think it a disgrace to shirk, but all the while his thoughts were on the luck gift.

"I wonder what it will be?" he said to his grandfather. They took turns at guessing, until it was time to feed the goats and house the chickens for the night.

A week later the man who had driven Johan and his mother away came by on his return from Vienna, and Franz fairly flew out to get his gift. "It is something very big," he called to the old frame-maker as he took a bulging bag. "See it is stuffed full!" And he expected to find something very wonderful.

But, when he opened it, he thought it wasn't wonderful at all. There was a blue velvet jacket, trimmed with gold braid and fastened with glittering buttons, such as Tyrolean boys wore in those days; and, in one of the pockets, he found a shining knife.

"Well, of all things!" he exclaimed as he held them up. "It's a splendid jacket, and the knife is a beauty, but I don't see where the luck part comes in."

But Hals Berner was old and wise, and a knowing smile played over his wrinkled face as he spoke. "It won't be the first time luck has hidden in a knife," he said, as he bent over his carving.

Franz did not know what he meant. He had always had a knife, for being of a carver's family, he was taught to whittle when he was a very little fellow and he had become remarkably skillful for one of his years. But no wonderful good fortune had come to him, and he was very sure that although each of the presents was nice, neither would bring luck, and he sent that word to Johan. But the brother wrote back from the city, "It will surely turn out to be a luck gift, Franz. Just wait and see." And still the boy wondered.

Winter came and icy winds blew down from the peaks. There was no word from Vienna now, for the valley was shut in by a glittering wall, and travel over the snow-drifted passes was impossible. There were other boys in the village, but each had his work indoors, and there was little time to play, so Franz had no chance for games. He helped his grandfather part of the day and sometimes whittled for his own amusement. It was a lonely life there in the hut with just the old frame-maker, who was often too busy to talk, so Franz was glad to do something to keep him busy. Now he made rings and tops and then just fantastic sticks or blocks.

One day as he whittled, his grandfather said, "Why don't you make an animal, Franz?" The boy looked up in surprise. "I don't think I can," he answered.

"Not unless you try," came the reply. "But, if you do that, you may surprise yourself."

Franz hated to have anyone think he was afraid to make an attempt, so he exclaimed, "I wonder if I could make a sheep?"

"Begin and see," the old man advised.

The boy went to work. At first it was discouraging. After many minutes of whittling, there was little to suggest what he had in mind. But then, with an occasional turn of the knife by the frame-maker and now and then a bit of advice, the boy began to see that a sheep would grow out of the block; and, when it did, he felt like a hero who had won a battle.

"It wasn't a bit hard, was it lad?" Hals Berner asked when it was finished.

And Franz agreed that it was not.

That was the beginning, and every day thereafter Franz worked at his whittling, and animal after animal grew under his knife. He was so busy he did not have time to be lonely, and had quite forgotten how sad he had felt over having to stay at home. It was such fun to see the figures come out of the wood and feel that he had made them. Of course they were crude, and not half so handsome as those his grandfather could have made; but anyone could tell what they were, and that was worth a great deal.

The *Parade of the Wooden Soldiers* by Jessel and the *March of the Toys* from *Babes in Toyland* by Victor Herbert have a jolly toy-like rhythm.

By spring he had a whole menagerie; and, when his mother came home, she found he had been a busy boy and a happy one as well.

"All made with the luck knife," Johan said as he looked over the work.

"So grandfather says," Franz answered. "It's a splendid knife, but I don't see where the luck comes in."

And again the knowing smile went over the old man's face.

One day soon afterward, his mother had word from the man who had been her employer in Vienna that his little son was not well and he was sending him to regain his health in the mountain air. A week later the child arrived with his nurse, and the first thing that attracted his attention was Franz's menagerie.

"Oh! Oh!" he exclaimed. "Dogs, cats, sheep, goats, lions, elephants, and all made of wood! I want them!"

"He means that he wants to buy them," his nurse explained. "Will you sell them, Franz?"

For a minute the boy hesitated. That menagerie had meant many months of whittling, and he loved every animal in it; and, if Johan hadn't interrupted, probably he would have refused.

"Why, Franz," the brother exclaimed, "it begins to look like a luck knife after all."

THROUGH FAIRY HALLS

That put a thought into his mind that caused him to answer, "Yes, take them. I can make some more."

So, when the child went back to Vienna, he took a wooden menagerie from the Tyrolean mountains. Other Viennese children, seeing it, wanted to possess one, and orders began to pour in to Franz, far more than he could fill. Then other villagers took up the work, until all over the valley people were making animals and toys.

The work grew to be a big industry, and toys from the Grodner Thal were sent all over Germany, and even to the lands beyond. One generation after another went on with the work; and, although it is two-hundred years since Franz began it, the craft continues there to this day. At Christmas time, shops in every land are filled with toys from the Tyrolean mountains; and, although they do not know the story, thousands of children have been happier because of a peasant boy's whittling.

So out of the bag sent back from Vienna, there came in truth a luck gift and it wasn't the fine jacket either, but the knife with which Franz whittled his first sheep. The boy had found out that luck doesn't mean something sent by fairies, but the doing a thing so well that it brings a rich reward; and, although he lived to be a very old man, he never got over being grateful that his mother made him stay behind when she and Johan went to the city.

The little valley among the Austrian Alps is still called Grodner Thal on the maps, but, because of the animals and toys that have come out of it, it is almost as well-known by another name. If you are good guessers, you can surely tell what it is, especially if you know that the peasants still speak of the lad who made the first menagerie there as the Luck Boy of Toy Valley.

The Boy Who Made His Own Materials

IN THE little village of Pieve di Cadore, under the tall, jagged peaks of the Dolomites in Italy, there lived, in the 15th Century, a boy named Tiziano Vecelli. Cadore was a quiet place high up in the mountains and, at sunset, when the great rocky pinnacles glowed rose pink all about, the old square of the town echoed to the homely tread of cows, the dainty clatter of goats, and the musical sound of the cowbell as well as to the deeper tones of the big bell in the church. Cadore was far out of the world, and Tiziano longed with all a boy's love of adventure to go down from that land of the sky to the queenly city by the sea—Venice, with her pink-and-white palaces on myriad little islands and her hundred beautiful bridges over winding canals. Tiziano wished to go to Venice, not only because the city was as beautiful as a dream city out of a fairy tale, but he wanted to go to Venice because of the great artists there who could teach him what he wished to know more than anything else in the world—how to paint like the masters. The great Bellini was there. To study under him was Tiziano's dearest dream. But Tiziano's father saw no good in dreaming. He was a well-to-do mountaineer, but a very practical man. Go away off to Venice—the very idea was wild!

"The thing for you, son," he said, "is to be apprenticed to Luigi, the cobbler. You shall learn to make good stout shoes!"

Still, in all his spare time, Tiziano drew pictures, using bits of charcoal and drawing on boards or stones. The villagers shook their heads. Only the village priest praised him. "No dream is impossible of fulfillment," said the good priest, "if one works with persistance and courage to make that dream come true."

So Tiziano continued to draw. But one thing troubled him greatly—all the pictures he made were black, drawn with his piece of black charcoal, yet round about him glowed a perfect glory of color—the beautiful blue of the sky; the delicate, changing pinks of the great jagged peaks above him; the green of the grass in the meadows; the red, blue, and yellow wild flowers; the golden brilliance of sunshine; and the rich, soft, mellowed tints in the old houses of the town. Color! Color! Color! Tiziano loved it more than anything else in the world. Yet how was he to reproduce it and get it into his pictures? He had no money to buy paints, and paints were expensive in those days. Antonio, his father, would never even listen to anything so foolish as buying paints for a boy when the family needed food and clothing and fuel to keep them warm. Let Tiziano make shoes! There was a trade for a man! All the same, Tiziano continued to dream of painting and to wonder if there was not some way he could make a picture in colors.

Now, every year in June, the people of Cadore celebrated with games and frolics and all sorts of merrymaking the Festival of the Flowers. So Tiziano and his sister, Catarina, went out into the meadows one day to gather flowers for the feast. Nowhere in the world can one find more beautiful wildflowers than on the sunny slopes or in the shady valleys of the towering Dolomites, and all the young people of the village went there to gather flowers. At sunset, they came home bearing armfuls of vivid blossoms, then they gathered together at the village inn to weave the flowers into garlands.

But, when the next day came, before the fun really started, Tiziano chanced to pass the spot where the garlands had been woven the evening before. Suddenly, he noticed stains on the stones of the walk before the inn. They were stains from flowers that had been dropped and crushed, and those stains were colored! They were every color, too! Every color a painter needed! Every color was there! In a moment the feast and the fun went out of Tiziano's mind. The villagers started dancing, but Catarina saw her brother heading away from the merriment and hastening out of the village. She ran to bring him back—for the two were fond of each other and she did not wish him to miss the fun—but, when she overtook him, she found him in a meadow like a variegated quilt for the brilliance of the wildflowers. "Tiziano! Tiziano!" she called, "Why are you running away from the feast?"

The boy did not answer for a moment. Too often he had been joked by his family and by the villagers for the crazy dreams in his head. But at last he answered bluntly, "I have found that the stains of flowers make colors and I am going to paint a picture."

For a moment the girl stood open-mouthed with amazement. Had he gone absolutely mad, or, could what he said be true? Then suddenly she felt overpowering all else, a yearning desire to help him if help there could possibly be to make his dream come true.

"I'll help you gather the flowers," she said. So together they picked the blossoms and, when their arms were full, they went to an empty stone house that stood on ground their father owned.

"Now leave me, Catarina, "Tiziano said, "I don't want even you to see my picture until it is finished."

Reluctantly, Catarina went back to the merrymaking, leaving Tiziano sketching with charcoal on a bare wall.

Thereafter for many days, the two young people kept their secret. Catarina gathered flowers in the meadows and brought them to the window of the house where Tiziano worked. Each petal made only the tiniest stain of color, but Catarina never failed

her brother. She kept him sup-
plied with blossoms, and Tiziano
painted with all the fire of genius.
At last, one evening, Tiziano said
simply, "It is finished!" And he let
the girl in to see what he had done.

Amazed she stood before the
magic transformation of a great
bare wall. There now in all their
splendor were figures of glorious
color! "Oh, Tiziano!" Catarina
said with reverence in her voice.
"It is a Madonna you have painted."

"Yes," he answered, "A Madonna and child with a boy
like me offering a gift. It is what was in my heart, Catarina."

When the girl had recovered from her astonishment and looked
her fill at the picture, she ran as on the wings of the wind to spread
the news through the village of what Tiziano had done. Soon
everyone in Cadore who was able to walk, run, or hobble was on
his way out to the house. Antonio, the boy's father, coming back
from a day's hunting, wondered what could be the matter that
there was such a crowd around his old stone house. Pushing his
way through the throng, he saw, above the heads of the people,
the great picture of the Madonna painted on the wall and his
own son, Tiziano, standing there before it.

"It is beautiful, so beautiful! How did you do it?" people said.

"I did it with flowers Catarina gathered," answered the boy.

Antonio was dazed. His son, his son that was to have been a
cobbler, his son had not only painted this beautiful picture,
he had made his own materials! He had made his dream come true!

So Tiziano did go to Venice and study under Bellini and, in
time, the boy of Cadore became the great painter Titian* whose
pictures have never been surpassed for the glory of their colors.

*Titian (1477-1576), one of the greatest of the Venetian school of painters, is famous for his rich color.
The *Assumption of the Virgin, Venus and the Lute Player* are well-known paintings by Titian.

The Strong Boy
A Canadian Tale

Once an Indian woman went on a journey with her infant son through the wild Canadian woods. And as she trudged along alone save for the baby slung on her back, there came from the woods a great Grizzly Bear. Seeing the woman with no one to guard her, the Bear growled fiercely, seized her in his great, shaggy arms and carried her and her son off to his dark cave in the mountains. There he kept them prisoners for years. They must live on what poor scraps of food he threw them and every night the woman must dance to his bidding, dance and amuse him until she was utterly worn out. And if ever she refused to dance, she got a cruel scratch from his claw or a cuff from his mighty paw. Nor did the woman and her son ever see daylight, for the Bear's five grizzly sons stood guard at the door of the cave when he was away from home.

THROUGH FAIRY HALLS

Well, in time the woman's son grew up into a fine strong lad. One day when he was twelve, he was sitting looking into a pool which was formed by a little stream that came bubbling into the cave. Then lo! he saw a Face peering up at him out of the water.

"What is the use of a boy who sits still and lets his mother be bullied?" said a Voice from the water.

"No use!" the Boy answered sadly. "I long to save my mother! But how can a boy like me overcome a great grizzly bear and his five grizzly sons?"

"You'll never overcome them if you sit still in this cave and don't even use what strength you have," said the Water Spirit. "You can only grow strong enough for such a deed by going out into the world and performing each day some task harder, requiring more effort and strength, than the task you performed the day before."

"But how am I to get out into the world?" asked the Boy. "The Bear's five sons forever stand guard at the only door!"

"Ah!" gurgled the Water Spirit. "Don't be too sure that's the only door! Slip out of the cave as I slipped in." And with another gurgle, the Face in the pool disappeared.

Then the Boy ran and told his mother what had occurred.

"My son," said the woman with a sadness as of tears in her voice, "the Water Spirit is right. The time has come when you must leave me and go out into the world to grow strong."

Just as they spoke, into the dark cave came the Bear. Fiercely he rose up on his hind legs and snarled to the woman:

"Dance! Dance, you! Dance till your teeth rattle! Dance!"

At that the Boy could stand it no longer. With a furious shout, he rushed on the Bear. Astounded by his sudden rebellion, the Bear stood for a moment with gaping mouth and paws poised high in the air. Then he grasped the Boy with his forelegs, meaning to crush the breath out of him. But he was a clumsy beast. With such force did he lunge against the Boy that he knocked the lad backwards into the pool. And the moment his own paws touched the water he started to howl, "Ow-ow! Ow-ow!" For the Water Spirit was stinging him with a stinging as of a thousand wasps. So the Bear loosed his hold on the Boy and jerked his paws from the water. Then the Boy was free at last.

The next thing he knew he was gliding along beneath a stream and the Water Spirit was beside him. Soon he saw ahead a glimmer and a shining. Then they were out of the dim, dark cave and came to the surface of the stream. For the first time within his memory, the Boy saw full sunlight. And he gasped with delight as he saw before him the great, wide, beautiful world. Guiding the Boy to the shore, the Water Spirit said:

"Go now and grow strong! And when you're ready to return and save your mother, jump in the river and call for me!"

So the Boy thanked the Water Spirit and off he went on his journey. He hadn't gone far when he met a man lifting a great canoe from the water. Just ahead in the stream were rushing, roaring, foaming rapids and the man was going to carry his canoe along the bank till he could launch it in the smooth water beyond the rapids.

"Let me help you," said the Boy.

But the Man, seeing he was only a lad, laughed with derision and jeered:

"Much help you'd be, little squirrel!" Then he turned the canoe upside down, lifted the front part to rest on his shoulders and said to the Boy, "Take hold of the other end, if you like. Perhaps you can lift as much as a grasshopper!"

So the Boy put his shoulders under the rear of the canoe and away they marched. Very heavy the canoe seemed to the Boy at first but as they went farther, he felt the burden less and less. Soon he was taking more and more of the weight till by-and-by the Man had shifted it all onto his shoulders and was only pretending to carry it.

THROUGH FAIRY HALLS

At last when they launched the canoe in the river below the rapids the Man said:

"You're surely a strong boy! Why don't you journey along with me?" For he thought to himself that he could make good use of such a strong fellow as this.

So they travelled on together. They travelled far and they travelled long. And every day the Man gave the Boy more work to do and did less and less himself. So every day the Boy grew stronger and stronger and the Man grew weaker and weaker.

One night they encamped at a place on the river where the current was powerful and swift. Scarcely had the Boy gathered the firewood and lit the fires, when they saw a large canoe filled with people come swirling madly along down the stream. The people had lost their paddles, so they could not control the canoe and the current was bearing it straight for the spot where the river plunged down in a mighty waterfall that would dash the canoe to pieces. Men, women, and children were frantically waving their hands, calling for some one to save them. At that, there came from the forest a great, burly man who bore a pole of enormous length. Running it out across the river, he held it above the canoe. Then the people in the canoe caught hold of the pole. And as they clung to it, the Man held them up, lifting them far above the water and trying to draw them to the shore.

"There's a strong man!" said the Boy to himself. But just then he saw that the Man's strength was failing. He was letting the pole slip down. In another moment he would drop it, the people would fall in the river and be swept away by the current. So the Boy seized the pole and, as the Man loosed his hold and sank down exhausted, the Boy pulled all those people, dangling, kicking, screaming, safely in to the shore. Then the burly man looked at the Boy with great admiration and said:

"You're a strong boy, lad! Let me journey on with you!"

So after that there were three of them paddling off down the stream together. They travelled far and they travelled long. But every day the Men shifted more and more of the work to the Boy and every day as he worked he grew stronger and stronger while the Men grew weaker and weaker.

Winters and summers they travelled. Then at last they went ashore one day to build a lodge where they could rest for a time. But the Men made many motions while the Boy did all the work. And when he had put up a comfortable lodge, the Men gave him orders every morning to go out and hunt to provide them all with food.

"We'll mind the lodge!" they said.

But while the Boy was gone, the two lazy Men lolled about all day, smoking their pipes and doing nothing. Only toward nightfall did they bestir themselves and cook supper. One evening they had just got supper ready when the thinnest, leanest, most starved looking little boy came to the door of the lodge crying bitterly and begging for food. So poor, so miserable, did he look that the Men bade him come in and help himself to a bite. But no sooner had the starveling seated himself to eat than in a twinkling he gobbled up all the food they had prepared. At that the Men were very angry and they fell on the little fellow to beat him. But the little fellow gripped them with hands of iron. Tiny as he was, he held those two strong men so they could not move a muscle. Banging their heads together, he gave them such a drubbing as they had never had before. Then he vanished and left them.

When the Strong Boy came home he found his two comrades sighing and groaning and heard the tale of the terrible little Imp who had stolen their supper and given them a beating.

"Tomorrow," they said to the Boy, "we'll go hunting and let you stay home!" For though they hated work, they much preferred going hunting to staying behind and running the chance of falling in once more with the Imp.

So off went the Men while the Boy stayed home, worked about the lodge and got the supper. When it was all cooked, there came the little fellow, crying bitterly at the door and begging for something to eat.

"Come in!" said the Strong Boy. At once the Imp came in and made a dive for the food. But the Strong Boy fell on him and held him fast. Then there was truly a struggle. The Imp had his strength by magic and was almost a match for the Strong Boy. They wrestled and tussled and tussled and wrestled. But at last the Strong Boy got the Imp down and sat on him. Then the Imp began screeching:

"Let me go! Let me go! I never thought there was anyone in the world strong enough to beat me. Let me go and I'll show you how you can use your strength to win great treasures of blankets and wampum."

"Nay!" said the Boy. "I have no wish to win treasures!"

"How then would you use your strength?" the Imp demanded.

"To save my mother from the Bear!" the Boy replied.

"But if you'll let me go," the Imp insisted, "I'll show you how to conquer a chief and rule all his tribe."

"I have no wish to conquer a chief and rule his tribe," said the Boy. "I wish only to save my mother!"

So when the Imp saw that he could not turn the Boy aside from the purpose for which he had got his strength, he knew that he could not rule him. As long as the Boy did not forget that it was to save his mother he had grown strong, there was nothing that could stand against him. So the Imp said:

"I yield! I've been enslaved by a terrible Giant who has never been defeated! If you can overcome the Giant and free me from him, I'll be your servant from this time on!"

So the Strong Boy let the Imp go free and off they went to the Giant's cave. When they went in, there stood the Giant looming up as big and dark as the shadow of a pine tree, cast by the moon at midnight. And he sprang on the Strong Boy like a whirlwind. For a day and a night they fought. But at last the Strong Boy overcame the Giant and slew him. Then the Imp willingly became the Strong Boy's servant.

But when the Strong Boy returned to the lodge with the Imp, his comrades, hearing how he had conquered not only the Imp but the Giant, began to think that he had grown too strong altogether. Now they were afraid of him because they were so much weaker than he. So when they set out again on the river they began to plan in secret how they could get rid of him.

At last the Men, the Boy and the Imp came to a place where the river ran into a narrow valley with great, dark cliffs towering up on either side. They wanted to land but the cliffs came straight down to the water's edge and they could find no place to beach their canoe. At that the Men said to the Boy:

"You stay here and we'll climb the cliff. Then we'll let down a rope and pull you up with the canoe."

So they climbed the cliff and let down a rope. Suspecting no evil, the Strong Boy was about to tie the rope to the canoe when the Imp cried:

THROUGH FAIRY HALLS

"Don't do that! You've grown so strong those Men are afraid of you now. They'll pull you half way up the cliff, then they'll let go of the rope and you'll fall crashing, to your death!"

So the Strong Boy got a huge rock and tied it to the rope, while the Men were too high above him to see what he had done. Then he called out, "Ready! Pull me up!" Well, they tugged and they tugged and when they had the rock half way up, sure enough, they let go, so the rock came crashing down and they thought they had rid themselves of the Strong Boy forever. But the Boy climbed up the cliff, and when the Men saw him safe and sound, they were so astonished and terrified that they ran for their lives and vanished into the forest.

Thus freed of his unworthy companions, the Strong Boy ran down to the river. At last, after all the strength he had gained, he felt ready to return to his mother in the cave. So he took the Imp by the hand, flung himself into the river and called on the Water Spirit. At once the Water Spirit came to his aid and soon all three of them were gliding smoothly along underneath the water. In less time than it takes to tell they came up in the Grizzly Bear's den. The Bear had just come home and he was standing up there in the darkness more ugly and threatening than ever.

"Dance!" he was snarling as usual to the poor woman. "Dance till your teeth rattle! Dance till your bones fall apart! Dance, I tell you. Dance!"

But the Strong Boy fell on him and seized him. It was a different story now from what it had been when they fought before, for in the Strong Boy's arms the Bear could scarcely move. He wriggled, he writhed, he struggled. He snarled, he growled, he howled. But the Boy only hugged him the tighter until he could scarcely gasp. Slowly but surely the Boy hugged the breath out of the Bear until at last he fell lifeless to the ground.

Meantime, the Bear's five sons, hearing all the noise, came rushing to aid their father. But the Imp kept them busy outside the cave. Striking swift blows at all five, he darted so quickly from one to the other that they kept twirling around in circles trying to catch him. Then the Strong Boy came and finished off each of them in turn, while the Imp continued to bedevil the others as long as there were any left.

Thus, having disposed of all his foes, the Boy returned to the cave, embraced his mother and led her out into the great, wide, beautiful, sunlit world which she had not seen for so many years. After that he built a good lodge for her and took care of her always, while the Imp and the Water Spirit lived happily close by.

The Man Who Loved Hai Quai

An Indian Tale of Mt. Tacoma

WHERE the pines loom dark against the sky, beneath the glistening snow peak of the great white Mt. Tacoma, there dwelt once a hunter. In the fragrant pine woods he followed the game; he fished in the rivers and in the placid lake where Tacoma stands upside down in the water. But more than all else he loved hai quai—glittering strings of shells—shell money—treasure, treasure, treasure. There came a time when he thought of nothing but hai quai. He would steal the lip-jewels of women, he would snatch little strings from the children's necks, and he longed to learn of some magic, by which he could heap up still more of the treasure. Ah, then the evil one came and dwelt in his heart and whispered to him always, "Hai quai! More hai quai!"

One day the hunter stood on the shore of the lake dreaming of shell money, when there came to him out of the forest, Moos-Moos, the great Elk, his *tahmahnawis* who watched over him.

"You want hai quai," said Moos-Moos. "Hearken, I know where you will find it, find it in great heaps, more than any red man has in all your lodges."

The hunter listened eagerly.

"Go to the very top of the mountain," said Moos-Moos. "Amid the snow on its peak you will find a valley cleft out of the rocks, and there lies a lake of black, black water. On the shores of this lake rise three giant rocks. One is like a salmon, one like the kamas root, and one like me, an Elk. Beneath the Elk's head, dig. There you will find hai quai, great shining strings of hai quai. And when you have it, show your thanks to the Great Spirit and to me by placing one string on each of the rocks."

"I will be rich! Men shall call me Great Chief!" cried the

hunter, and he bade farewell to the Elk and went back to his lodge. "I go away on a long hunt," he said to his squaw. Then he seized his elk-horn pick and set forth.

Through the dense forests he climbed, by the side of rushing mountain brooks, over flowery upland meadows, among mighty rocks, where the snow began, past gnarled and twisted trees that grew on the edge of the timber, and so on up into the everlasting snows. Then darkness overtook him. It was bitter cold. He rolled himself in his blanket and lay down to sleep. In his sleep he dreamed. He had strings and strings of hai quai hanging about his neck. Tighter they grew and tighter, tighter and tighter. Ah! they were choking him. With a wild cry, he awoke. It was only a dream, and still he wanted hai quai.

Before the sun, he was up and on his way once more. Just as dawn glowed rosy over the snow, he reached the mountain top. There before him, as Moos-Moos had said, was the lake of black water and, rising from it, the giant rocks of the salmon, the kamas root, and the Elk. Seizing his pick, he began at once to dig at the foot of the rock that was shaped like the Elk. All day long he worked, digging, eagerly digging, and twelve great otters rose up out of the strange, dark waters to watch him.

Just as the sun was sinking he came upon the treasure, great heaps of glittering hai quai. His eyes glowed like fire; from his lips came weird sounds like the laughter of a loon; deep down into the shining shells he dug his hands. He slipped the strings over his neck, his arms, he clutched them tight to his bosom. He held them up to the light to catch the last gleam of the setting sun. He thought not of Moos-Moos, nor of the Great Spirit, to offer thanks. He hung no strings on the rocks, but clutching them tighter and tighter, he started off down the mountain.

Then the otters uttered a strange, sad cry and dove down into the waters, and Tootah, the thunder, in answer, went crashing across the sky. The wind began to howl and shriek, snow came swirling fiercely down. And still the hunter clutched his treasure tight and struggled on and on.

The storm increased, the wind roared, Tootah, the thunder, seemed rending the very heavens. Then the hunter took one single string of shells and cast it grudgingly to the winds. "For the Great Spirit," he said. But as he hugged his treasure the storm burst more furiously on him. The night and the mountain found voices and on every side they shrieked in his ear, "Hai quai! Hai quai! Hai quai!"

One by one, he cast his precious strings away, and he groaned as he did so, as though he gave up a part of himself. At last they were gone, those shining strands—he flung the last one from him. Then he fell to the ground, exhausted, and his eyelids closed in sleep.

When he awoke the sun was shining and in his heart was a wonderful peace. He found himself at the foot of a tall fir tree, the same beneath which he had dropped the night before, and, above, the great white mountain smiled graciously upon him. He was hungry but as he started to rise, he found his limbs were stiff, his clothing was in rags and from his head hung hair as white as the snow on Tacoma. Astonished, he looked about him. All was the same as it had been the night before, and yet somehow it was different. He dug some roots to eat and then started slowly down the mountain.

He thought now no more of hai quai. In his ears was the song of birds, in his eyes the golden glow of the sun through the soft smoky haze of Indian summer, and in his heart calmness, utter peace, like the calmness of the mountain, majestic and serene.

At length he came to a lodge before which sat a squaw. She was old and her hair was white. He knew her not and passed her by, yet no! She called him back. Her voice was glad and sweet, and lo! it was his own wife and his own lodge! Not two

short nights, but years and years had passed since he left her.

"How many moons you have been gone!" she cried. "I have traded much since you went and made much hai quai. I will give it all to you."

"Nay," said the old man. "Give me a seat by the lodge fire and a welcome. I care not for hai quai, I care only for peace!"

Then the good squaw was astonished.

Henceforth the old man sat at his lodge door, pondered much, and gave friendly greeting to all who passed him by. To those in need he gave hai quai, to those in trouble he gave good counsel, and to old and young who sought his advice, his answer was always skokum (good).

So he was much beloved, and there dwelt, evermore undisturbed in his heart, the wisdom, peace and quiet that he learned from the great white Tacoma.

THROUGH FAIRY HALLS

"IT"*
JAMES WHITCOMB RILEY

A WEE little worm
in a hickory-nut
   Sang, happy as he could be,
"Oh, I live in the heart of the
      whole round world,
And it all belongs to me!"

THE MICE
A WINNEBAGO FABLE

ONCE some mice lived under a log;
   They had never been anywhere else,
So they thought
That place was the world.
They thought that they
Were the only people in all the world.
One of them stood on tiptoe;
He stretched his little arms up until
He was able to touch the under side of the log.
He thought he was very tall
And that he had touched the sky;
So the little mouse danced and sang:
      "Throughout the world
      Who is there like little me?
         Who is like me?
      I can touch the sky.
      I touch the sky, indeed."

*Copyright used by special permission of the Bobbs-Merrill Company.

The Lost Spear
A South African Tale

ONCE there lived in South Africa a King who ruled a tribe of powerful black men. One day he called all his Chiefs together to witness a contest between the four strongest, bravest and handsomest youths of his tribe. Then he announced:

"That one of these four who can throw his assegai the farthest shall have my youngest daughter, Lala, for his wife."

Now three of these young men were sons of great Chieftains, but Zandilli, the fourth, was only a poor herdsman. Yet the lovely Princess Lala, who stood looking on, thought him the best of all, for he was a splendid big fellow with broad shoulders and mighty rippling muscles. Soon the champions started to throw. The first threw his assegai so well it fell upright into an ant hill far, far away. The second sent his spear, quivering, into a fir tree many paces beyond the ant hill. The third pierced the breast of a gold-and-green sugar bird that was fluttering over an aloe blossom still farther away. But Zandilli, the herdsman, who was fourth, threw his assegai with such strength that it flew up into the heavens and struck a hawk soaring high in the sky.

Loud were the acclamations of the Chiefs and the people. One and all, they adjudged Zandilli the winner while the Princess laughed for joy.

But the King did not wish his daughter to wed a humble herdsman. Angrily he said: "This man's weapon was surely bewitched! Let the youths throw again tomorrow with spears that I shall give them!"

So the next day the King gave all four of them spears of gold. But to the Princes he gave equally-balanced ones while he gave the herdsman one unbalanced, untrue of aim. Yet Zandilli's assegai again outdistanced those of the others. It flew so high it was lost to sight in the clouds above the towering peaks of the mountains. In a rage the King cried: "You shall have my daughter only if you find your assegai and bring it here to me." For well enough he knew that to find a spear lost in the clouds above the mountains was an impossible task.

Loudly Lala wept, but the King said sternly:

"Stop weeping! 'Tis for me to decide whom you shall wed!"

So Zandilli, who loved Lala deeply, set out in search of his assegai. For three days he wandered through the wild mountains, vainly seeking his spear. Then on the fourth day he paused a moment, looking down into one of those cool brown mountain pools that he loved. And as he stood there, a butcherbird dropped at his feet, clutching a frog in his talons. The frog cried for help and Zandilli, filled with compassion, took it from the claws of the bird. Then the frog, full of gratitude, croaked, "If you're ever in trouble call for me! At a single sigh from you, I'll come to your assistance!" And with that he dived into the water and disappeared from sight.

A little farther on Zandilli saw a large black and yellow butter-fly. Caught by one of its beautiful wings on the thorn of a prickly pear, it was fluttering helplessly and tearing a larger hole in its wing. So Zandilli, halting, released it with tender care. And the butterfly, as thankful as the frog had been, said, "Youth! Kind youth! If you're ever in difficulty call on me! I'll come to your aid at once!" Then the butterfly flew away.

On the fifth day, darkness came while Zandilli was still wander-ing. And the moon, which should have given him light, was hidden by fog in the east. So Zandilli, anxious to find some shelter for the night, entered a narrow gorge through which trickled a tiny stream. It was very dark in this ravine. Its walls were high, he fell in deep water-holes and stumbled over slippery boulders. But in spite of the difficulties Zandilli persevered, knowing how often caves are to be found in these ravines. Then at last the moon rose in all its beauty, clear of the drifting fog. Floating high in the sky, it shone down into the gorge, sending a pathway of silver straight into the mouth of a cave.

Boldly Zandilli entered that cave. But the moonlight was not yet reaching far into it and Zandilli was too weary to explore the black shadows beyond. Lying down, he closed his eyes and for a little time he slept.

When he awoke the cave was in total darkness but a strange, soft music greeted his ears, music softer and sweeter than the murmur of the wind among the grassbells. Its sound thrilled Zandilli's heart and drew him irresistibly toward it. So he arose and crept with steps as noiseless as the leopard's toward the place whence the music came. As he advanced, the cave grew broader and higher and a pale light seemed to flood the walls. Louder grew the music at each step, loftier the walls, and more brilliant the light until, suddenly, such a sight burst upon his astonished eyes as never mortal had seen before.

THROUGH FAIRY HALLS

Before him lay a large lake, as deeply blue as a sapphire. Above him, the roof of the cave shone brightly, upheld by great pillars, which sparkled as with millions of diamonds. And in the center of the lake, on a little island, a glistening flight of steps led up to a throne, which sent forth flashes of green fire, as if it were made of emeralds.

To Zandilli the lake seemed boundless, its shores were lost in darkness. But from the shadows in all directions countless white water lilies came floating, each bearing toward the throne a small being in the shape of a very tiny woman. It was from these lilies the lovely music floated, for each tiny woman was singing as she came. Never had Zandilli seen such beautiful beings. More delicate did they seem than the soft windflowers that crown the slope of a cliff. Their faces and arms were white, their hair, which floated behind them, was as brilliant as the fiery tail of the great star, which comes to warn black men of approaching drought, and their brows were crowned with star-blossoms. From all sides, the lily boats floated and as they touched the small island with the glistening steps in the midst of the sapphire blue lake, the Little People stepped from their boats and joined throngs of others, like themselves, who stood in shining glory around the emerald throne.

All this Zandilli saw, his eyes large with wonder. Only who it was that sat up there on the throne he could not see, for that Being was hidden from him by a shimmering misty veil of light. Then suddenly the music ceased. The Little People parted and through their midst that Being, clothed in shimmering light, came down from the throne to the water's edge, calling out in a silvery voice, "Zandilli, we expected you! Come across to me!"

At that a canoe of gold shot from the base of the steps and came to rest before Zandilli. Fearlessly he entered it and, quick as light, he was carried across the lake.

Then as he stepped from the canoe, he saw that the dazzling Being before him was a lovely woman. From her hair, her face, her silvery robes shone brilliant rays of light. She sparkled as diamonds sparkle and she, too, wore a crown of star flowers. Placing her hand on his arm, she said:

"Welcome to the land of the Moon-People!" Then she took his hand, led him up the steps and seated him beside her on the emerald throne.

"Zandilli," she said, "I know that you seek a golden spear and that you hope to win a beautiful King's daughter as your bride. Now the moon has risen five times since you vanquished the Princes in throwing the spear. Once more after tonight, she will shine over land and sea. Then at dawn of the following day your Princess will be forced to wed another unless you return with the spear!"

"O great Queen!" Zandilli cried. "Tell your servant how best he can serve you and find the spear!"

"The spear is within your reach," the Queen replied. "It fell at the mouth of this cave and was placed in our treasure trove. Would I could say it is yours for the taking! But the wisest beings among us are the Star-Men. Long since they foretold the coming to us of a mortal in search of a weapon he valued most highly. And they have decreed that that mortal should not have his weapon back until he has proved himself worthy of it by performing two difficult tasks. These tasks he must fulfill successfully or he must die. And you, Zandilli, are that mortal. So I go to consult my Star-Men concerning the tasks to be set you before you can have your spear. Meanwhile, my attendants will show you the beauties of our home."

With these words the Queen arose. Below her, empty lily boats dotted the lake, as water lilies dot the quiet reaches of rivers, floating lazily backwards and forwards. And the Queen, descending the steps, got into one of these boats and was borne swiftly off out of sight.

Then three of the loveliest of the Moon-Maidens stepped with Zandilli into the golden canoe. Off they drifted across the sapphire blue lake.

And now wonder after wonder unfolded itself to the herdsman's astonished gaze. For from the lake narrow, glistening little waterways led into chamber after chamber, each of which seemed more magnificent, more glittering, more sparkling than the rest. Thus they went until at last they came, most unexpectedly to Zandilli, to a dark, ugly room where the walls were black as night. A frowning, threatening, room! Zandilli shivered. But he shrugged off the creepy feeling it gave him, for he was thinking most of how the Princess Lala would be given to another man if he did not return with the spear before the second dawn. So he urged the Moon-Maidens to take him back to the Queen and they found her again on her emerald throne. Rising, she said:

"Zandilli, the Star-Men and I have decided on your first task. You have seen the black chamber! It is the one dark, ugly spot in our home. If you can make it as bright and beautiful as the other rooms, half your task will be fulfilled. But if you cannot accomplish this before dawn, you must die in accordance with the orders the Star-Men have given."

So Zandilli was taken to the black chamber. There he was left alone in the golden canoe with despair in his heart. He had thought that the Queen and the Star-Men would set him a task demanding some show of physical strength and manly power before they gave him back his spear. And in these things he excelled. Such a task he knew he could have accomplished. But, no! They had ordered that he must make this dark room beautiful and shining or he must die.

"I must die!" he thought. And he remembered sadly all the lovely things in the world which he would never see again—the beautiful Lala, the flowers, the birds and the butterflies! Butterflies! All at once he recalled the butterfly he had saved from the thorn. And he muttered, "O butterfly, if only you could help me now!" But that thought seemed hopeless. Wearily Zandilli laid himself down and slept. But the butterfly heard its savior's cry for help. It called together its brethren and its cousins, the fireflies. Quietly they all flew into that dark cavern. When Zandilli awoke he was astounded to find the dull walls about him shining and all transformed with a glory of bright colored wings. For the butterflies and the fireflies had spread themselves over all those walls and the fireflies were flashing with a million brilliant sparkling little lights. When the Queen and her followers came at dawn to see if the task had been performed, they marveled at the beauty before them.

"The Mortal has won! He has won!" the Moon-People cried.

THROUGH FAIRY HALLS

Then they took him back to the island in the lake where they danced all day. But at evening the Queen rose and said:

"Mortal, you have completed your first task! So the spear is partly won. Here it is on the steps before my throne!" And there on the steps Zandilli saw it, the golden assegai. But the Queen then went on, "The robes of my attendants are made from the shining gossamer wings of flies and our storerooms are empty of wings. So this is to be your second task—you must fill a hundred of our boats with the wings of flies ere the moon sets this night or you must die!"

Then the Queen and her attendants disappeared, leaving Zandilli in the golden canoe on the lake, surrounded by a hundred empty canoes. Again he felt utterly discouraged, for this task seemed even more hopeless than the first. And he sighed to himself, "Never more will I see the sun! Never more will I hunt the leopard! Never again will I see the tumbling mountain streams nor that cool brown pool where I saved the frog from the butcher-bird!" Thinking these sad thoughts, he fell asleep in the boat at last. But the frog heard the sigh of the man who had saved him. So he called his brethren and his friends, the lizards. And they all caught flies and more flies. Soon they had filled the hundred boats with the shining gossamer of flies' wings. Awakened by their busy croaking, Zandilli found his task performed. And when the Queen saw all those boats full of the shimmering delicate gauze of flies' wings she cried to Zandilli, "The spear is yours!"

Then she took Zandilli back to the island and gave him his golden assegai. Jumping into the canoe, he propelled it with his spear to the edge of the lake. There he bounded ashore. Racing the coming dawn, he rushed to the hut of the King. And he arrived just in time, for the King was about to give Lala to a Chief's son. But at sight of the assegai, he had to keep his promise. He gave Lala to the herdsman and those two lived happily ever after.

Jack the Giant-Killer

AN ENGLISH FOLK TALE

WHEN good King Arthur reigned, England, despite all the efforts of the valiant knights of King Arthur's Round Table, was troubled by many giants who did most terrible deeds in the land. It was in those days that there lived near Land's End in the County of Cornwall, a farmer who had one only son, Jack. Jack was a bold, brave lad and of a very ready wit, so that nothing and nobody could get the best of him.

Now out in the sea beyond Jack's home rose a rocky island called the Mount of Cornwall. And on that island dwelt a huge giant named Cormoran who was the terror of all the nearby villages. He lived in a cave in the midst of the Mount and whenever he wanted food he would wade across the stretch of sea, which came scarcely above his ankles, then when he reached the mainland, he would snatch whatever he wanted.

At his approach all the people ran before him while he seized their cattle, making nothing of carrying half-a-dozen oxen at a time on his back. As for their sheep, he would grab them by handfuls and tie them around his waist till they hung there like nothing more than a string of tallow candles. For many years he had done this so that all Cornwall was in despair.

But when Jack was of an age to understand these things, he had no mind to run from the giant. So he went to his father and said very boldly:

"This Cormoran has troubled the land long enough! 'Tis time he was slain! And I'm the fellow who means to go forth and slay him!"

"Nay, nay!" the father cried in great distress. "This you must not do, my son! For if you go forth against the giant, 'tis you who'll be slain! Remember you're only a farmer boy, having no weapon at all with which to fight a giant! You're not like the knights of the Round Table who have fine swords to fight with!"

"No matter!" quoth Jack. "I shall do very well without a sword!"

So he got a horn, a shovel, and a pickaxe, and on a dark evening, he rowed quietly to the Mount. There he took his shovel and started to dig. Before daylight he had dug a pit twenty-two feet deep and nearly as broad, covering it over with sticks and straw. Then he strewed dirt on top of it all so it looked like the rest of the ground. After that he placed himself on the opposite side of the pit, farthest from the giant's lodging. Just at the break of day, he put the horn to his mouth, and blew it.

"Tantivy, Tantivy!" he blew.

Well, of course, that noise woke the giant up. Rushing from his cave, he saw Jack and cried:

"Villain! You villain! You've disturbed my rest! I'll make you pay dearly for this! I'll take you and broil you for my breakfast!"

But no sooner had he spoken, than he tumbled into the pit. And so big was he that he made the very foundations of the Mount to shake.

"Ho, ho!" laughed Jack. "Where are you now, Oh, Giant? What do you think at this moment of broiling me for your breakfast?"

And he raised his pickaxe, gave the giant a mighty whack on the head and killed him on the spot. Then he filled up the pit with earth and searched the giant's cave, where he found much gold and other treasures which Cormoran had stolen.

Now when Jack got back to town he found all the magistrates in the town-hall, holding council as to how they could rid the land of the giant. And they were so happy at hearing Jack had already slain him, that they not only told him to keep all the treasures he had found but declared that he should henceforth be known as—

JACK THE GIANT-KILLER

THROUGH FAIRY HALLS

Then, to the youth's great delight, they presented him with a fine sword and a splendid belt, on which were embroidered in letters of gold:

> *Here's the right valiant Cornish man,*
> *Who slew the giant Cormoran.*

After that Jack, having plenty of treasures from Cormoran's cave to keep his mother and father in comfort, decided to leave them and finish off a few more giants who were plaguing King Arthur's land. So he said good-bye to his parents and off he went, tramping along and along and along on the road that led toward Wales.

Already the fame of his victory over Cormoran had spread across all West England. So a giant, named Blunderbore, hearing of it, took a mighty vow to be revenged on Jack if ever he should catch him.

Now Blunderbore was lord of a castle situated in the midst of a lonesome wood. And Jack, having walked a long, long way without any sleep, was nearing this wood when he sat down to rest by a pleasant fountain. Then, being very, very weary, he fell asleep, though it was not yet mid-day.

Well, while he was sleeping, Blunderbore, coming to the fountain for water, discovered him and learned from the lines written on his belt that this was the far-famed Jack the Giant-Killer. Without more ado, he picked Jack up, slung him over his shoulder and went off with him, tramp, tramp, tramp, carrying Jack to his castle.

When Jack awoke, he was fast in the clutches of the giant. Needless to say, he shivered and shook for a time and he didn't feel any easier in his mind when Blunderbore took him into his castle and he saw the courtyard there all strewed with human bones.

"Ere long your bones will lie with these!" the giant bellowed. "For I mean to eat you for supper!"

Then he locked Jack in an immense room on an upper floor while he went to fetch another giant, his brother, to share in the meal on Jack.

For some time Jack waited, then he went to the window and looked out. Far off he saw the two giants coming.

"Now," quoth he to himself, "my death or my deliverance is at hand."

And searching about his room, he found in a corner two strong ropes. Taking these, he made a noose at the end of each. Then looking out of the window again, he saw that the giants were just below him, unlocking the gate of the castle. Quickly he threw out his ropes so a noose fell over the head of each. Then he drew the other ends across a beam in the room and pulled with all his might till he had those giants dangling by their necks with their legs jerking in the air. At that he slid down one of the ropes, out the window and on, till he reached the giants when, drawing his sword, he cut off their heads.

Taking the keys of the castle from the giant who had owned it, he went through the place from cellar to attic, unlocking door after door. And in one of the rooms he opened he found three fair ladies tied by the hair of their heads to hooks in the wall and almost starved to death.

"Sweet ladies," quoth Jack, when he had released them. "I have destroyed this monster and his brutish brother! You are now free!"

Then, when the ladies had rejoiced and thanked him, he proceeded on his journey.

He had come into Wales when it chanced that he got benighted and could find no habitation where he might sleep. However, he came at last into a narrow valley, where he found a large house and knocked at the gate. But what was his surprise when the gate was opened by a monstrous giant with two heads! Yet despite his two heads, this giant did not appear so fiery as the others had. For he was wily, covering his secret malice under a false show of friendship. Very pleasantly he greeted Jack and showed him with many kind words into a chamber where he might sleep. But in the dead of night, Jack heard him saying in the next room:

"Though here you lodge with me this night,
You shall not see the morning light.
My club shall dash your brains out right!"

"So that's the sort of trick you're up to!" quoth Jack. "Well, I hope to be clever enough to thwart you!"

And he laid a big stick of wood in the bed under the covers where he had been sleeping. Then he hid himself in a corner of the room.

Soon the giant came in and seeing the covers all humped up as though Jack lay under them, he struck several mighty blows on that hump with his club, after which he left the room, thinking that he had broken every bone in Jack's body.

Next morning he was astounded when Jack turned up for breakfast whole and gave him hearty thanks for his night's lodging.

"How—now tell me how—how did you rest last night?" the giant stammered. "Did you feel anything, anything at all?"

"Nay!" quoth Jack, "I felt nothing but a rat, which gave me two or three slaps with her tail!"

Well, the giant was now completely bewildered. But he thought to get rid of Jack by setting him a task he could not perform. So he brought in a mountainous hasty pudding and said:

"Friend, dear friend! 'Tis my pleasant custom to serve every guest in my house with such a fine pudding as this! 'Tis most delicious, I assure you! But whoever proves himself to be such a weakling that he can't eat it all, must of course be put to death for you know as well as I do, that little no-good worms have to be stepped on and crushed so they'll no longer litter the earth!"

Larger than twenty men could eat that pudding was! So Jack excused himself for a moment and went to his room. There he dumped his belongings out of the large leather bag in which he carried them on his travels. Placing the bag over his belly but under his loose coat, he arranged it in such a way that he could slip spoonfuls of pudding into it when he seemed to be carrying them to his mouth. Then returning, he sat down at the table with the giant and managed to make it appear that he was eating all the pudding when the truth was that by far the greater part of it was going into that bag. And when to the giant's amazement he had disposed of all the pudding, he said boldly:

"I'll show you a trick!" And taking a knife, he ripped it across his front as if he were slitting his belly though it was only the bag he was cutting. Then before the giant's very eyes out came all the hasty pudding.

"You see!" said Jack. "I can safely rip my own belly open. That's a trick you can't do!"

But the giant wasn't going to be outdone by any little whipper-snapper.

"Odds splutters!" he cried. "I can do that trick too!"

And seizing the knife, he ripped open his belly and fell down dead.

So having now disposed of five giants, Jack went on his way again.

Now, it happened at this time that King Arthur's only son set out for Wales to visit a beautiful lady with whom he was deeply in love. But the demon, Lucifer, had cast a spell over the lady, so that at times she seemed as one crazed and did only Lucifer's bidding. Very deeply the young Prince wished to free her from the demon's spells.

He was going along in Wales when he fell in with Jack and told the sad story to him.

At once Jack asked permission to accompany the Prince on his mission. To this the Prince agreed. He got a horse for Jack and the two rode off together.

When the sun got low that evening the Prince said:

"Jack, we should find ourselves lodgings for the night. But there's not a house in sight!"

"Rest easy, sir!" Jack replied. "I have a cousin who lives within two miles of this place. 'Tis true he's a giant with three heads! And 'tis true that, alone by himself, he can fight five hundred men in armour and put them all to flight! But he'll give us beds for the night."

"Nay!" cried the Prince. "That's no place for us to lodge! Your cousin would certainly chop us up at a mouthful!"

"Wait and see!" quoth Jack. "Let me go ahead to prepare the way. And do you stop here till I return!"

Then Jack galloped off with a thunder of hoof beats and when he came to the gate of the castle, he knocked so loud that he made the neighboring hills resound.

"Who's there?" roared the giant.

"Only your poor cousin, Jack!" Jack answered. "And, Cousin, I come in haste, for I bring you bad news!"

"Bad news!" the giant snorted. "What bad news can there be for me? Have I not three heads? Can I not fight five hundred men in armour, and make them all fly like chaff before the wind?"

"Aye, aye!" quoth Jack. "But, Cousin, I've just seen a King's Son coming with a thousand men in armour! A thousand, Cousin! They're coming here to kill you and then destroy your castle!"

"A thousand men in armour!" The giant was terrified. "That's bad news indeed! Five hundred I can handle! But a thousand! A thousand will kill me! Cousin, I must hide myself with all haste! Come with me to my secret room! Then lock, bolt and bar me in, and keep the keys until the King's Son is gone!"

So Jack, going along with the giant, locked, bolted and barred him in a vault beneath his cellar. Then Jack went and fetched his master and they made merry whilst the giant lay trembling in his vault.

Next morning Jack rode off for three miles with the Prince. Then thinking that his master was far enough away so the giant could not catch the smell of him, Jack rode back and let the giant out of his vault.

"Cousin," the giant cried, "you've saved my life! You've saved my castle! How can I reward you?"

"Why," Jack answered, "Just give me that old coat and cap,

those slippers and the rusty sword which are beside your bed."

"Cousin, Cousin!" the giant cried. "You know not what you ask! You ask the most precious things I own! For the coat will keep one invisible, the cap will tell all one wants to know, the sword cuts asunder whatever it strikes, and the shoes are of extraordinary swiftness. Yet but for you I would have been slain! So I'll give you these things gladly!"

Then he got the coat, the cap, the sword and the shoes and gave them to Jack. Jack thanked him for them, left the castle and rejoined his master.

After that they arrived very soon at the house of the lady with whom the Prince was in love. The lady was very fair. She received the Prince most lovingly and that evening she had a fine banquet spread before him and Jack. But when they had eaten there suddenly came to her eyes a crazed look and Jack knew that the evil demon, Lucifer, now possessed the poor maiden's mind and spirit. Rising she kissed the Prince on his lips but in a manner far from loving. Then she cried out in a voice that was piercing and shrill:

"Tomorrow morning you must show me the lips I kissed last tonight or my headsman will cut off your head!"

"That will be no difficult task if you kiss no lips but mine!" the Prince replied. "For I'll show you my lips!"

But at that the lady gave a crazed sort of laugh and said:

"As to whose lips I shall kiss last, that's something I'll leave you to guess!" And off she went to her room.

Then the Prince was dismayed and in great sorrow. But Jack's Cap of Knowledge told him what to do and where the lady would go. So he put on the Coat of Invisibility and the Shoes of Swiftness and flew through the night to the dread abode of Lucifer. Standing beside the demon, all unseen because of his magic coat, he waited for a little time. Then in came the poor crazed maiden, for Lucifer had drawn her to him that he might destroy the young Prince she loved. As though in a trance, the maiden bent over and kissed the demon. Then off she went again. No sooner was she gone than Jack took out his magic sword and cut off Lucifer's head. Carrying it under his invisible coat, he took the head back to the Prince. So the next morning when the maiden demanded that the Prince should show her the lips which she had kissed last the night before, the Prince brought out Lucifer's head and held it up by the horns before her. Then the young lady laughed and cried all at once. And she knew that she was free of the demon's enchantments forever. Most lovingly she kissed the Prince and they were married at once.

The next day all three set out for the castle of King Arthur. And the King was so pleased, not only with the help Jack had given his son, but with all his exploits in ridding the land of so many giants, that he made Jack one of the Knights of the Round Table.

THROUGH FAIRY HALLS

And now while Jack spent a fortnight as a knight among knights at King Arthur's court, he saw there a maiden lovelier than he had ever seen before. She was the daughter of a Duke and Jack wished with all his heart that he could have her for his wife. But before he could speak out his love, a terrible thing occurred.

One night there appeared in the sky above the Duke's castle a flaming chariot drawn by fiery dragons. And the next morning the lovely daughter of the Duke was nowhere to be found. So everyone knew that some evil creature, having the powers of enchantment, had carried her off in that flaming chariot. Grieving greatly, Jack set off at once to find her.

Soon he came to a cave, near the entrance to which a huge giant was sitting with a big knotted club by his side. The giant's goggle eyes flamed with fire, his countenance was ugly, the bristles of his beard resembled heavy iron wires and the locks that hung down on his brawny shoulders were like curled snakes or hissing adders.

Alighting from his horse, Jack put on the Coat of Invisibility, went up close to the giant and said:

"Oh, is it you here? Well, it won't be long before I take you fast by that pretty beard of yours!"

Not being able to see Jack because of his coat, the giant began to swat about with one huge paw as though he thought buzzing flies were trying to bother him.

Then Jack drew his sword and struck a blow at the monster's head, but missing aim, he cut off the giant's nose instead of his head. At that the giant roared like thunder, seized his huge club and began to lay about him like one stark mad. But Jack, running behind him, drove his sword up to the hilt in the giant's back, so he fell down dead.

This done, Jack cut off the giant's head, and finding a waggoner, he hired the man to carry the head, with his compliments, to King Arthur.

Then, taking the giant's keys, he went on into the cave to see if perchance the Duke's Daughter was hidden there, for he meant to overlook no place where she might possibly be imprisoned. Through many windings and turnings in the cave he walked and he saw piled up in one chamber much gold and many treasures. But nowhere was there a single sign of the Duke's Daughter, his beloved.

Finally he came to a very large room where a caldron was boiling over a fire and against one wall of the room stood the enormous table at which the giant had been accustomed to eat.

Just beyond this, the great cave came to an end with a chamber that had a barred window. And through the window Jack beheld a vast number of miserable captives, who, seeing him, cried out:

"Alas, young man! Art thou come to be one amongst us in this terrible den? For we are those whom the giant fattens here for his feasts. Each day he takes from amongst us the fattest, whom he slays and cooks in his caldron!"

"Well, the giant will have no more of you in his caldron!" Jack answered. "For this day I have slain him!"

Then he unlocked the door and let the rejoicing captives out, but they were all men. The Duke's Daughter was not among them.

So Jack divided the treasure of the cave equally among all present including himself. Then he went on his way.

That evening he came to a castle where he sought lodging for the night and the owner proved to be a very pleasant knight. He took Jack in gladly and invited him to eat at a table where many other knights and ladies were feasting. Sitting down with the guests, Jack asked first of all if any of them knew aught of the whereabouts of the Duke's Daughter. But none of them could tell him anything about her.

The next morning he was just about to set out again on his journey, with the knight and his guests all at the gate to bid him godspeed, when a frightened messenger came dashing up on horseback.

"Sir!" he cried to Jack. "Thunderdell, a terrible giant with two heads, has heard how you killed his kinsman at the cave. And he's come from the northern dales to take vengeance on you! He's within a mile of the castle, with the country people flying like chaff before him!"

"Well let him come!" cried Jack, deciding at once to delay his departure. "Aye, let him come, for I have tools to pick his teeth! Ladies and gentlemen," he turned to the other guests, "if you'll go to the walls of the castle you'll witness Thunderdell's death and destruction!"

Now the castle was situated on a small island that was surrounded by a moat thirty feet deep and twenty feet wide, and the waters of the moat were spanned by a drawbridge. So Jack employed men to take saws and cut through this bridge on both sides nearly up to the middle, making their cuttings show as little as possible and leaving intact only so much of the bridge as would bear the weight of a man his size. Furthermore, he ordered that six horses should be harnessed together and held ready for his bidding. Then donning his Coat of Invisibility, he crossed the bridge while the knights and ladies lined up on the wall above. Soon the giant appeared. Though he could not see Jack he could smell him. And he cried out fiercely:

> "*Fee, fi, fo, fum!*
> *I smell the blood of an Englishman!*
> *Be he alive or be he dead,*
> *I'll grind his bones to make me bread!*"

"Say'st thou so?" said Jack. "If thou canst grind my bones to flour thou'lt prove thyself to be a more able miller than I think thee!"

At that the giant cried out again:

"I'll tear thee with my teeth! I'll suck thy blood! And no matter what thou sayest, I'll grind thy bones to powder!"

"But first thou must catch me!" quoth Jack. And throwing off his Coat of Invisibility so Thunderdell might see him, he ran from the giant, who followed him as heavily as though he had been a walking castle. For a long time Jack, who was wearing his Shoes of Swiftness, led the giant a merry chase, slipping out from under his very hand or out of reach of his club just as Thunderdell thought he had him. Meantime, the knights and ladies on the castle wall laughed heartily at this sport.

THROUGH FAIRY HALLS

At last to end the matter, Jack ran lightly over the draw-bridge, with Thunderdell pursuing him at full speed. But when the giant reached the middle of the bridge, his enormous weight broke it down. Headlong he tumbled into the water where he rolled and wallowed like a huge whale.

Quickly Jack flung two ropes over the giant's two heads, then he fastened the other ends to the six horses which were waiting and had them haul him ashore.

And when Thunderdell was on the bank Jack cut off his two heads and ordered that they should be sent to King Arthur.

After that he went on his way in further search of his beloved. By-and-by he came to a lonesome house and knocked at the door which was opened by an old man with hair as white as snow.

"Father," said Jack, "can you lodge a benighted traveller?"

"Aye!" the old man answered. "Thou art right welcome to my poor cottage!" And he took Jack into the house where the two sat down together. Then the old man said:

"Son, I see by thy belt that thou art the famous and mighty conqueror of giants! And behold, on top of this mountain lives Galligantua, the most terrible of all giants. By the help of a conjurer, this Galligantua has tricked many knights and ladies into his castle. There by magic art they are transformed into birds or beasts. Poor things! I grieve for them, every one! But above all, I grieve for a certain lovely young Duke's Daughter!"

Now when Jack heard these words—a certain lovely young Duke's Daughter—he pricked up his ears.

"They fetched her from her father's garden in a fiery chariot," the old man went on. "And up there in the castle, they changed her into a little white doe. Oh, my son, would that thou couldst save her! But brave though thou art, I doubt if even thou couldst get into that castle, for its gates are guarded by two fire-breathing griffins, which destroy every one who comes near!"

"Speak on!" Jack cried. "I'll surely save the maid!"

Then the old man said, "Well, son! Shouldst thou be able to get past those griffins, thou'lt find engraved in large letters on the gates of the castle how the spell may be broken."

So Jack thanked the old man heartily and early on the following morning he put on his Coat of Invisibility, his magic cap and shoes, and started out on his way. As soon as he reached the top of the mountain he saw the two fiery griffins, but he passed them safely, because he was invisible. And when he had got beyond

THROUGH FAIRY HALLS

them, he found on the gates of the castle a golden trumpet hung by a silver chain, under which these lines were engraved:

> *"Whoever shall this trumpet blow,*
> *Shall soon the giant overthrow,*
> *And break the black enchantment straight;*
> *So all shall be in happy state."*

At once Jack took the trumpet and blew it. And at the terrible blast he blew, the gates swung open while the whole castle shivered and shook as though an earthquake had struck it. Then Jack passed through the gates into a courtyard where he saw all manner of birds and beasts, they being the knights and ladies who had been enchanted by the wicked conjurer. And among them, trembling with fright, was a lovely little white doe, whom Jack knew to be the Duke's Daughter, his beloved. There too were the giant and the conjurer, biting their nails and tearing their hair, for they knew their wicked reign was over.

Wishing to meet face to face this giant who had stolen his beloved, Jack threw off his Coat of Invisibility.

Then the giant seeing him, seized his club and rushed on him. But Jack raised his sword and at one blow he cut off Galligantua's head. Thereupon the conjurer, seeing that he had lost his powerful protector, gave an awful scream, mounted up into the air and was carried away in a whirlwind.

And no sooner had the conjurer disappeared than all his wicked enchantments were broken. The castle vanished in a cloud of smoke. All the birds and beasts became knights and ladies and the lovely little white doe became once again Jack's beloved, the beautiful daughter of the Duke. Gladly she gave Jack a kiss. And with the whole party rejoicing, they set out for King Arthur's court.

When they reached there the King was so overjoyed at all Jack had accomplished that he heaped the highest honors on him. And the Duke gave Jack his daughter in marriage. All the Knights of the Round Table came to dance at his wedding. And Jack and his lady lived happily all the rest of their days.

The Duty That Was Not Paid*
KATHERINE DUNLAP CATHER

More than a hundred years ago a man and his two children were journeying from their home in Salzburg to Vienna. They traveled by the Danube boat, and Marianne, the sister, stood by the rail tossing pebbles into the water and watching the turbulent river swallow them up. Her dress was worn almost threadbare, but her face was so sweet and her eyes were so large and bright that she looked pretty for all her shabbiness.

Just behind her on the deck her father and brother were talking. "If we make some money in the city you'll buy sister a new dress, won't you, Father?" little Wolfgang asked.

Marianne whirled and started toward him. She knew that was sure to make her father sad, and she called, "Don't coax, Wolfgang. My dress will do very well until we can afford to buy another, and a new one will seem all the nicer because of my having worn this one so long."

Her brother turned his big, earnest eyes upon her, and said, "But, Marianne, I know you want one. I heard you wish for it by the evening star, and last night you put it in your prayer."

Father Mozart turned from them with a sad look on his face,

*Used by special arrangement with the author and the publishers, David C. Cook Publishing Co.

and walked up and down the deck, wishing very much he could do what Wolfgang asked. But he was just a poor orchestra conductor with an income so small he had to stretch it hard to provide food and shelter for his family. Marianne must wear the shabby frock until better times began, which he hoped would be soon. They were to give some concerts in the Austrian capital, and maybe in that rich, music-loving city would earn enough to make them more comfortable than they had been before. But until then they must not spend a penny save what was needed for food and shelter, because the customs fee on the harp they carried must be paid, and that would reduce their little fund to a very small amount.

Wolfgang, too, thought about it as the boat crept in and out between the hills, and wondered much if there was no way in which Marianne might have the dress before they played in Vienna. His old teacher in Salzburg had often told him that there is a way out of every difficulty if one is clever enough to think of it, and there must be out of this. His own suit was bright and new, for his birthday was just past and it had been his uncle's gift. But Marianne was a very shabby little girl, and he knew she was unhappy though she was brave and sweet about it.

They were gliding past the ruins of the castle that once, men said, had been the prison of Richard the First, England's Lion-Hearted King, when his enemies took him captive on his return from the holy wars. Often in the twilight time at Salzburg, as they waited for the father to come from his work, the mother told them his tale.

"He was very brave and wise, too," the boy thought as he looked at the crumbling pile. "He would have found a way for Marianne to have a new dress if she had been his sister."

Was it the prayer being answered, or just the fulfillment of the wish made by the evening star? For while he thought, an idea came into his head. It was a good idea, it seemed to him, so good that it made him smile. If it worked out, and he believed it would, Marianne might have the dress she wanted so much, because then his father would have more money to spend.

Just to the south they could see the great spire of St. Stephen's, a tall, gray finger against the sky, which told that Vienna was not far away. As it grew nearer and nearer, looming up bigger and plainer before them, Wolfgang thought more and more of his idea, until when they reached the mooring his eyes were dancing and his cheeks were aflame. His father believed the thought of seeing the great capital had excited him, but that was not it at all. He had a secret plan and could hardly wait until he knew whether or not it would work out.

The journey was ended and the people were going ashore. "Please loosen the cover, Father," he said as Leopold Mozart carried the harp toward the customs gate.

"Ah, you are proud of it!" the man answered with a smile.

Wolfgang did not reply, thinking what a poor guesser his father was. He watched him as he set the instrument down and undid the wrapping, bringing the polished frame and glistening strings into full view. Then he went over and took his place beside the harp as the customs officer drew near, and Marianne came and stood beside him. She had forgotten all about her dress in her eagerness to find out how much duty they would have to pay.

"What have you to declare?" the man asked.

"Only a harp," Leopold Mozart answered, as he laid his hand on their one treasure.

"It is a beautiful instrument and valuable," the official said as he looked at it, and named as the price of the duty an amount so big as to cut their little hoard almost in half.

Father Mozart's face grew very serious, and the merriment

went out of Marianne's eyes. But Wolfgang did not worry. He still had that idea in his mind, and believed it would work out.

Leopold Mozart reached into his pocket for the little sack containing his savings, but it was not necessary to open it, for just as he was about to do so, Wolfgang started to play. The customs officer turned with a start and listened, and the people, gathered there, forgot all about duty charges as they crowded around the little musician. His tiny hands swept the strings as if his fingers had some magic power, and the melody they made was sweeter than ever heard on that old wharf. For five minutes, ten, he kept at it, and there was not a whisper or a murmur, only a sort of breathless surprise that one so young could play so wonderfully.

"What!" one exclaimed as he finished, "a lad of his age to perform like that!"

"Yes," the father answered with a smile, "he does well at the harp."

"Amazing," the officer murmured, "I've heard many a good harpist in my day, but never anything sweeter than that."

Wolfgang smiled. The idea was working out, and he was very glad. Already he had visions of a happy sister in a handsome new gown, and turning again to the instrument, he played even more beautifully than before, for the gladness that crept into his heart was creeping also into the music.

For some minutes he picked the strings, while the people listened as if held in a spell, until the father said, "We must go now, for it is getting late, and we have yet to find lodgings in the city." And he handed the money to the officer.

But the man shook his head. "No," he said, and his eyes were very tender. "A boy who can give as much pleasure as that deserves something. Keep the money and buy a present for him."

As Wolfgang heard the words he gave a bound. "Father"

he exclaimed, with sparkling eyes, "buy the dress for Marianne. You can do it now, since you have saved the customs money."

The officer looked at him in amazement. "He is a wonderful lad, truly," he exclaimed, "and as kind as he is wonderful!"

"Yes," came the low reply. "He has wanted nothing so much as a new dress for his sister."

And she did get it, too, a beautiful one of soft, bright red, all trimmed with shining buttons. Wolfgang danced with delight when he saw it, and there was no happier child in all Vienna.

They gave many concerts there, some before the royal family; and Maria Theresa, the empress, became greatly attached to both brother and sister, gave them handsome clothes and beautiful gifts, and forgot all about affairs of state while Wolfgang played. She called him the "little sorcerer," and agreed with the customs officer that he was a wonderful child.

Then, after some weeks, they went back to the home in Salzburg, where the boy kept on at his music, doing such marvelous things that his fame traveled far. He grew to be the great master, Mozart, at whose glorious music the world still wonders, and he was a generous and sweet-souled man, just as he was a big-hearted and thoughtful child. Many lovely acts are told of him, but none that shows his kindness and tenderness in a more delightful way than when as a boy on the Vienna wharf he charmed the customs officer and all others who heard, and Marianne got the dress for which she had wished with the duty money that wasn't paid.

Wolfgang Mozart (1756-1791), began composing music when he was seven. Brought up in the court life of Austria, he is famous for his delicate, stately minuets, such as the "Minuet" from the opera, *Don Giovanni*.

The Wonderland of an Artist's Workshop*

YOUNG Giovanni wanted more than anything in the world to paint. Little rascal though he was not above skylarking and chattering like a monkey, he still had that great urge—he wanted to be a painter. There were big brushes made of pigs' bristles and little brushes made of squirrels' hairs set in a goose quill. His fingers itched to handle them all, to lay on beautiful colors, to make bare walls or pieces of wood blossom with living figures— men and women, horses and dogs, trees and flowers and birds!

It was a thrilling world in which Giovanni lived—the Italy of the 15th Century. Men were alive and doing. They were questioning, seeking, discovering. Only a few years before, Columbus had sailed from Spain and found a whole new world. There was adventure in the air! And down in Florence, men were exploring, as though it had been a new world, the possibilities of painting.

Why, two-hundred years before, artists painted people flat as though they'd been made of paper, with no good stout flesh and bones and muscles beneath their clothes. They would give a poor, little Christ child two left feet with the big toe on his right foot where the little toe ought to be. And, if they painted twenty angels, all twenty looked just alike without a grain of difference or character in their faces. There they stood in a row, all in the front of the picture, for artists had no idea how to paint some in the distance grown little as things appear when they are seen far away. How to make bodies round, how to give faces expression, how to paint some figures near and some far and farther away— all this the artists of Florence had worked out, step by step.

And now there had been working for some years in Milan, the city where Giovanni lived, a great artist come from Florence, Leonardo da Vinci. He had painted, for the monks of St. Dominic on the walls of their dining-hall, a picture of Jesus at the Last Supper with his disciples grouped around him. Every disciple

*In Da Vinci (1452-1519), and Michelangelo (1475-1564), Italian art reached its peak. Starting 200 years before with no knowledge of painting real forms, Florentine artists mastered every problem of painting what they saw.

showed a different expression of face so one knew from looking at them just what each thought and felt, who it was loved Jesus best and who it was would betray him. It was a glorious picture.

Nothing would do for Giovanni but to study under da Vinci.* So off he went one day to seek the master's workshop. Leonardo, himself, met the lad at the door. What a tall, imposing figure with his thick, light hair and long, fair beard!

"So here's a lad would learn to paint," said Leonardo kindly, although he looked at the boy out of keen blue eyes under frowning brows. "Art thou willing to work and to work hard, my Giovanni?"

"Aye," answered Giovanni eagerly.

In another moment, the boy found himself in the master's bedroom. Other boys were there in the light of a blazing fire that flamed from a great brick hearth, all busy with paint or crayons. Leonardo gave Giovanni a flat iron-scraper and set him to smoothing a panel of wood to be used for painting a picture. Then the master talked to the boys about preparing oil to mix the colors; for, before Leonardo's time, men had mixed paint with eggs and they could not with such a hard mixture get all the fine play of light and shade that shows the expression on human faces. Leonardo it was who had introduced the use of oil. Giovanni worked and listened with a deep thrill in his heart that now, at last, he was here to be taught by the great Leonardo.

Now and then he peeped into the adjoining workshop. What a room that was! By the flame of a candle and the light from a great smelting furnace, the boy could see a place cluttered up with machines, wheels, levers, springs, screws, pipes, and metal shafts. Now what were such things doing in the workshop of an artist? In one corner, was a huge crystal representing a human eye. There was the skeleton of a horse; a huge, stuffed crocodile; pointed, boat-shaped skiis for walking on the water; and the small clay head of a girl with a sly and dreamy smile. There was everything

*Da Vinci's perfection in painting what he saw has governed methods in art until today, when men begin to paint what they imagine and perceive with their minds as well as what they see with their eyes.

under the sun for delving into problems of mechanics as well as art. Was that what it was to be an artist, to search into all the questions of the universe? Most astounding of all to the curious young Giovanni, there, reaching from floor to ceiling, was a great thing like a bat with four enormous wings made of shiny, starched taffeta and a feathered tail like a bird. What in the world could that be? Giovanni stared with all his might. And, tinkering away at the thing, there stood an enormous man, a veritable giant, his simple, childlike face covered with soot and grime.

When the first day's work was over, Giovanni could scarcely wait to ask the other boys about that strange machine.

"'Tis the master's flying-machine," answered one of the lads. "He has been trying for years to make a machine that would fly."

"Aye," laughed Marco, another boy. "There's nothing will hold him to earth. He's really crazy enough to believe that men can fly. He's forever studying the flight of wasps and bees and flies and whatever soars in the air. You'd have thought he had found a fortune he was so overjoyed when he learned that insects steer themselves by using their hind legs as rudders! There's no question in the universe he doesn't try to answer!"

"And that big fellow, Astro," a third boy interrupted, "he is the master's mechanic and he's as crazy as the master about this matter of flying. When they first came to Milan, what did he do one day, when Leonardo was away from home, but take the thing up on the roof. The master had forbidden him to try it; but Astro wound his body with great, big bull and pig bladders blown up full of air to float him if he should fall. And he put his feet in the stirrups and began to work the cords attached to the blocks and levers that move the wings. The big bat began to flap. Up it went for a little, then down it came, smash, in a heap! If Astro hadn't landed in a heap of manure, he would have been killed by the fall."

"Aye," put in Marco, laughing, "all the bladders on Astro burst with a noise like thunder when he hit the earth."

The boys all joined in the laughter, but Giovanni was entranced. What a place this was, this workshop of the master! A beehive of mental activity! A powerhouse, generating ideas!

And what a man was the master! Now he was painting feverishly absorbed in seeing a picture come to life on his easel.

Now for days at a time, he would study nothing but cats—how they played, fought, slept, arched their backs, and bristled at dogs or calmly sat on their haunches, washing their mouths with their paws.

Now he was wandering around the town with a notebook in his hand, sketching scowls and smiles and all the varied expressions of people as they passed.

Now, in the depths of his study, he secretly pored over the dead body of a criminal which, it was whispered about, he had managed to get from the hangman when it was taken from the gallows; for he, first of all the artists, studied the human body in order to paint it more accurately.

Today, as though he were indeed no more than ten years old, he made little waxen animals that flew when blown up with wind, or he gave a pet lizard horns and a beard and made it a pair of wings, that trembled when it walked. Then he laughed like a boy to see how it looked like a dragon and he kept it confined in a box as a monster to frighten his friends.

Next, he was up in the dovecote, his hair shining gold in the sunlight while the white pigeons settled around him. Whoosh! He raised his arms, scattering the birds to the winds, then he joyously watched their flight as they soared on their outspread wings up into the air.

And often at night in the workshop, lit by the great smelting furnace or perhaps by a single candle with only a tomcat for company, he tinkered on his machine or studied the laws of mechanics and problems of mathematics.

In 1498, he had a new idea. He would make a new flying-machine, modeled on the flight of the swallow. Soon the great bat was gone and there, in its place in the workshop, Giovanni saw a great swallow made of taffeta stretched on reeds.

Astro was overjoyed. He hoped and yet he feared. Leonardo took so long to work out all the details and pronounce the machine complete, that Astro grew impatient. He wanted to try the bird.

"Master," he demanded bluntly, "will we fly or will we not?"

Seeing how tense the man was between his hope and his fear, Leonardo had not the heart to answer he did not yet know.

"One cannot know without making an experiment," he answered, "but methinks, Astro, that fly we will!"

One day soon after this, Leonardo left the house, and, when he was coming home after a few hours absence, he saw from far off a crowd of people gathered around the place. Hastening his steps, he pushed his way through the crowd and there he came on a sight that moved him to the heart.

Giovanni, Marco, and the other boys, all very grave of mien, were carrying a wing of the giant swallow and on it lay, strangely still, the blood-stained form of Astro, his eyes closed, his face deathly pale, and all his clothing torn.

That which Leonardo feared had happened! Astro had tried the machine. He had made its wings flutter a little and then he had fallen to the ground. Indeed, he would have been killed, had not one of the wings caught on the branches of a tree.

Sadly Leonardo helped the boys carry Astro into the house and put him to bed. With great concern, he bent over to inspect the wounds of the smith. Then Astro came to himself.

"Forgive me, master," he whispered.

There was always something exciting in the workshop of Leonardo. Giovanni and the other boys not only learned to paint there, but they learned to think and inquire and investigate the universe. And, though Leonardo left no machine that would really fly, he left his great painting of the Last Supper in Milan and an urge to vigorous thought which gives wings to the human spirit.

The Wise Men of Gotham

Three wise men of Gotham,
They went to sea in a bowl,
And if the bowl had been stronger,
My tale had been longer.

In old days the village of Gotham was known throughout all merry England, for that its men were wondrous wise.

On a time, twelve wise men of Gotham went a-fishing. Some went into the water and some fished on dry land. As they ambled home at nightfall, says one to the others, "We have been venturesome this day, comrades, a-wading in the brook. A marvel is it if none of us was drowned!"

"Aye, marry!" says another. " 'Twere well to count ourselves lest, peradventure, one of us was drowned and is now missing! Twelve of us did come from home."

So every man did count the others, man by man, and did never count himself!

"Lauk-a-mercy-on-us!" they all began to cry. "Here be but eleven. One of us is drowned!"

So they ran back to the brook, and looked up and down, and here and there with outcries and loud lamentations.

Anon, came riding by a gentleman. "Save you, sirs," says he. "Why all this dreadful dole?"

"Alas, good master," cried the wise men. "This day there came twelve of us to fish in this brook, and one of us is drowned!"

"Bless me!" says the gentleman. "Count yourselves, then, man by man!" And each did count eleven and never count himself.

" 'Twere pity of my life if one among so wise a company were lost," says the gentleman. "I pray you, what will you give me an I find the twelfth man?"

"All that is in our wallets," said the men of Gotham.

THROUGH FAIRY HALLS

So they gave the gentleman all the money they had; then he began with the first and gave him a whack on the shoulders with the flat of his sword, so he shrieked aloud. "That is one, by your leave!" says he, and he served them all likewise, counting them man by man. But when he was come to the last, he gave him a most dreadful whack, so he scarce held his footing. "By my faith!" cried he. "Here is your twelfth man!"

"Marvelous!" cried all the company. "Marvelous past the wit of man! You have found our neighbor that was lost!"

The next day but one, there went to market to Nottingham to buy sheep, a certain man of Gotham, and, as he crossed over Nottingham bridge, he met another man of Gotham going home.

"Where are you going?" asked he that came from Nottingham —Dobbin by name.

"Marry," says Hodge that was going to Nottingham. "I am going to buy sheep."

"And which way will you bring them home?" says Dobbin.

"Over this bridge," says Hodge.

"Not so, neither," says Dobbin. "I like not to have sheep cross over this bridge."

"Beshrew me!" says Hodge, "but I will bring them over the bridge an I choose!"

"By my life, but you will not!"

"I will!"

"You will not!"

"Rascal!"

"Rogue!"

And they fell a-beating their staves one against another as if there had been an hundred sheep between them.

"Have a care!" cried Hodge. "What with all this noise, my sheep will jump off the bridge!"

"It matters not!" shrieked Dobbin. "They shall not cross!"

"If thou makest so much to do, I'll put my fist in thy face!"

"And I'll put my staff on thy pate!"

As they were thus at contention, there came by another man of Gotham with a sack of meal on his horse. Seeing his neighbors thus at strife about sheep when there were no sheep between them, he said, "How now, stupid fellows, will you never learn wisdom? Peace! Peace!" Then he took down the sack of meal from his horse, went to the side of the bridge, opened the mouth of the sack, and shook all his meal out into the river.

"Look you, sirrahs," says he. "How much meal is there in my sack?"

"Marry!" said they. "None at all!"

"By my faith," says he. "There's even as much meal in my sack as wit in your heads, to be at strife about nothing! Let this be a lesson to you!"

And he went on his way with his empty sack, looking most marvelous wise.

LITTLE SHEPHERD'S SONG
William Alexander Percy

THE leaves, the little birds and I,
The fleecy clouds and the sweet, sweet sky,
The pages shining as they ride
Down there, down there where the river is wide!
Heigh-ho what a day! What a lovely day!
Even too lovely to hop and play!

And so I lie in the deep, deep grass,
And watch the pages as they pass,
And sing to them as they to me,
Till they turn the bend by the poplar tree.
And then—O then, I sing right on,
To the leaves and the birds and myself alone!

—13th Century

The Three Sillies*

JOSEPH JACOBS

ONCE upon a time there was a farmer and his wife who had one daughter, and she was courted by a gentleman. Every evening he used to come and see her, and stop to supper at the farmhouse, and the daughter used to be sent down into the cellar to draw the ale for supper. So one evening she had gone down to draw the ale, and she happened to look up at the ceiling while she was drawing, and she saw a mallet stuck in one of the beams. It must have been there a long, long time, but somehow or other she had never noticed it before, and she began a-thinking. And she thought it was very dangerous to have that mallet there, for she said to herself, "Suppose him and me was to be married, and we was to have a son, and he was to grow up to be a man, and come down into the cellar to draw the ale, like as I'm doing now, and the mallet was to fall on his head and kill him, what a dreadful thing it would be!" And she put down the candle and the jug, sat herself down and began a-crying.

Well, they began to wonder upstairs how it was that she was so long drawing the ale, and her mother went down to see after her, and she found her sitting on the settle crying, and the ale running over the floor. "Why, whatever is the matter?" said her mother. "Oh, mother!" says she, "look at that horrid mallet! Suppose we was to be married, and was to have a son, and he was to grow up, and was to come down to the cellar to draw the ale, and the mallet was to fall on his head and kill him, what a dreadful thing it would be!" "Dear, dear! what a dreadful thing it would be!" said the mother, and she sat her down aside of the daughter and started a-crying too. Then after a bit the father began to wonder that they didn't come back, and he went down into the cellar to look after them himself, and there they

*From *English Fairy Tales*. Used by permission of the publishers, G. P. Putnam's Sons.

two sat a-crying, and the ale running all over the floor. "Whatever is the matter?" says he. "Why," says the mother, "look at that horrid mallet. Just suppose if our daughter and her sweetheart was to be married, and was to have a son, and he was to grow up, and was to come down into the cellar to draw the ale, and the mallet was to fall on his head and kill him, what a dreadful thing it would be!" "Dear, dear, dear! so it would!" said the father, and he sat himself down aside of the other two, and started a-crying.

Now the gentleman got tired of stopping up in the kitchen by himself, and at last he went down into the cellar too, to see what they were after; and there they three sat a-crying side by side, and the ale running all over the floor. And he ran straight and turned the tap. Then he said: "Whatever are you three doing, sitting there crying, and letting the ale run all over the floor?" "Oh," says the father, "look at that horrid mallet! Suppose you and our daughter was to be married, and was to have a son, and he was to grow up, and was to come down into the cellar to draw the ale, and the mallet was to fall on his head and kill him!" And then they all started a-crying worse than before. But the gentleman burst out a-laughing, and reached up and pulled out the mallet, and then he said: "I've travelled many

 miles, and I never met three such big sillies as you three before; and now I shall start out on my travels again, and when I can find three bigger sillies than you three, then I'll come back and marry your daughter." So he wished them good-bye, and started off on his travels, and left them all crying because the girl had lost her sweetheart.

Well, he set out, and he travelled a long way, and at last he came to a woman's cottage that had some grass growing on the roof. And the woman was trying to get her cow to go up a ladder to the grass, and the poor thing durst not go. So the gentleman asked the woman what she was doing. "Why, lookye," she said, "look at all that beautiful grass. I'm going to get the cow on to the roof to eat it. She'll be quite safe, for I shall tie a string round her neck, and pass it down the chimney, and tie it to my wrist as I go about the house, so she can't fall off without my knowing it." "Oh, you poor silly!" said the gentleman, "you should cut the grass and throw it down to the cow!" But the woman thought it was easier to get the cow up the ladder than to get the grass down, so she pushed her and coaxed her and got her up, and tied a string round her neck, and passed it down the chimney, and fastened it to her own wrist. And the gentleman went on his way, but he hadn't gone far when the cow tumbled off the roof, and hung by the string tied round her neck, and it strangled her. And the weight of the cow tied to her wrist pulled the woman up the chimney, and she stuck fast half-way and was smothered in the soot.

Well, that was one big silly.

And the gentleman went on and on, and he went to an inn to stop the night, and they were so full at the inn that they had to put him in a double-bedded room, and another traveller was to sleep in the other bed. The other man was a very pleasant fellow, and they got very friendly together; but in the morning, when they were both getting up, the gentleman was surprised to see the other hang his trousers on the knobs of the chest of drawers and run across the room and try to jump into them, and he tried over and over again, and couldn't manage it; and the gentleman wondered whatever he was doing it for. At last he stopped and wiped his face with his handkerchief. "Oh, dear," he says, "I do think trousers are the most awkwardest kind of clothes that ever were. I can't think who could have invented such things. It takes me the best part of an hour to get into mine every morning, and I get so hot! How do you manage yours?" So the gentleman burst out a-laughing, and showed him how to put them on; and he was very much obliged to him, and said he never should have thought of doing it that way.

So that was another big silly.

Then the gentleman went on his travels again; and he came to a village, and outside the village there was a pond, and round the pond was a crowd of people. And they had got rakes, and brooms, and pitchforks, reaching into the pond; and the gentleman asked what was the matter. "Why," they said, "matter enough! Moon's tumbled into the pond, and we can't rake her out anyhow!" So the gentleman burst out a-laughing, and told them to look up into the sky, the moon was there and it was only the shadow in the water. But they wouldn't listen to him, and abused him shamefully, and he got away as quick as he could.

So there was a whole lot of sillies bigger than the three sillies at home. So the gentleman turned back home again and married the farmer's daughter, and if they didn't live happily ever after, that's nothing to do with you or me.

THE MERMAN
ALFRED TENNYSON

I

Who would be
A merman bold,
Sitting alone,
Singing alone,
Under the sea,
With a crown of gold
On a throne?

II

I would be a merman bold,
I would sit and sing the whole of the day;
I would fill the sea-halls with a voice of power;
But at night I would roam abroad and play
With the mermaids in and out of the rocks,
Dressing their hair with the white sea-flower;
And holding them back by their flowing locks
Laughingly, laughingly;
And then we would wander away, away,
To the pale-green sea-groves straight and high,
Chasing each other merrily.

III

There would be neither moon nor star;
But the wave would make music above us afar—
Low thunder and light in the magic night—
Neither moon nor star.

THROUGH FAIRY HALLS

We would call aloud in the dreamy dells,
Call to each other and whoop and cry
    All night, merrily, merrily.
They would pelt me with starry spangles and
        shells,
Laughing and clapping their hands between,
    All night, merrily, merrily,
But I would throw to them back in mine
Turkis and agate and almondine;
    Laughingly, laughingly.
O, what a happy life were mine
Under the hollow-hung ocean green!
Soft are the moss-beds under the sea;
We would live merrily, merrily.

Daniel in the Lions' Den
From the Book of Daniel

It pleased King Da-ri′us to set over the kingdom of Bab′y-lon an hundred and twenty princes which should be over the whole kingdom; and over these three presidents, of whom that Daniel who was of the captives of Judah, was first, that the princes might give accounts unto the presidents, and the king should have no damage. Then this Daniel was preferred above the presidents and princes because an excellent spirit was in him, and the King thought to set him over the whole realm.

Then the presidents and princes sought to find occasion against Daniel concerning the kingdom. But they could find none occasion nor fault, forasmuch as he was faithful, neither was there any error or fault found in him.

Then said these men, "We shall not find any occasion against this Daniel, except we find it against him concerning the law of his God."

Then these presidents and princes assembled together to the King and said thus unto him:

"King Darius, live forever! All the presidents of the kingdom, the governors and the princes, the counsellors and the captains, have consulted together to establish a royal statute and to make a firm decree, that whosoever shall ask a petition of any God or man for thirty days, save of thee, O King, he shall be cast into the den of lions. Now, O King, establish the decree, and sign the writing, that it be not changed, according to the law of the Medes and Persians, which altereth not."

Wherefore King Darius signed the writing and the decree.

Now when Daniel knew that the writing was signed, he went into his house; and his windows being opened in his chamber toward Jerusalem, he kneeled upon his knees three times a day, and prayed and gave thanks before his God as he did aforetime.

Then these men assembled, and found Daniel praying and making supplication before his God. Then they came near, and spake before the King concerning the King's decree:

"Hast thou not signed a decree that every man that shall ask a petition of any God or man within thirty days, save of thee, O King, shall be cast into the den of lions?"

The King answered and said: "The thing is true according to the law of the Medes and Persians which altereth not."

Then answered they and said before the King:

"That Daniel which is of the children of the captivity of Judah regardeth not thee, O King, nor the decree that thou hast signed, but maketh his petition three times a day unto his God as aforetime."

Then the King was sore displeased with himself that he had given assent to such a law. And he labored till the going down of the sun to deliver him.

But these men assembled unto the King and said unto him:

"Know, O King, that the law of the Medes and Persians is that no decree or statute which the King establisheth may be changed."

So the King commanded and they brought Daniel and cast him into the den of lions, and the King spake and said unto Daniel:

"Thy God whom thou servest continually, he will deliver thee."

Then a stone was brought and laid upon the mouth of the den, and the King sealed it with his own signet, and with the signet of his lords; that the purpose might not be changed concerning Daniel.

But the King went to his palace, and passed the night fasting; neither were instruments of music brought before him, and his sleep went from him.

And the King arose very early in the morning, and went in haste unto the den of lions. And when he came to the den, he cried with a lamentable voice unto Daniel. And the King spake and said to Daniel:

"O Daniel, servant of the living God, is thy God whom thou servest continually able to deliver thee from the lions?"

Then said Daniel unto the King:

"O King, live forever! My God hath sent his angel, and hath shut the lions' mouths, that they have not hurt me; forasmuch as before him innocency was found in me; and also before thee, O King, have I done no hurt."

Then was the King exceeding glad for him, and commanded that they should take Daniel up out of the den. So Daniel was taken up out of the den, and no manner of hurt was found upon him, because he believed in his God.

And the King commanded and they brought those men which had

accused Daniel, and they cast *them* into the den of lions; and the lions had the mastery of them.

Then King Darius wrote unto all peoples, nations and languages, that dwell in all the earth:

"Peace be multiplied unto you! I make a decree, that in every dominion of my kingdom, men tremble and fear before the God of Daniel; for he is the living God, and steadfast forever, and his kingdom that which shall not be destroyed, and his dominion shall be even unto the end. He delivereth and rescueth, and he worketh signs and wonders in heaven and in earth, who hath delivered Daniel from the power of the lions."

So this Daniel prospered in the reign of Darius, and in the reign of Cyrus, the Persian.

The Fairyland of Science*

THERE goes that lad, Henri, barefooted, bareheaded, his soiled smock flapping against his heels. He is coming home from the tiny hamlet of Malaval, where he has been living with his grandma and his grandad, horny-handed folk who till the soil. A solitary place it is, the cottage of Malaval, standing lone amidst the broom and heather, with no neighbor for miles around. Sometimes thieving wolves come sneaking by, and the country round about is a wild solitude of mossy fens and marshes oozing with pools. But Henri remembers how cozy the house is, how its barnyard swarms with lambs and geese and pigs, how its big room glows with the light from the fire, which brings into bright relief the eager faces of children, crowding around the table. Each child has a spoon and a wooden bowl before him; and there, at one end of the table, his unclipped hair like a shaggy mane, sits Grandad, cutting with vigorous stroke an enormous rye loaf the size of a cartwheel. Armed with a long metal ladle, Grandma is dipping the supper from a capacious pot that bubbles lustily over the flames. Um, how good it smells, the savor of bacon and turnips!

After supper, Grandma takes up her distaff and spindle in the corner by the hearth and tells the children stories as they squat in the firelight before her, stories of dragons, fairies, and wolves.

Henri loves these stories, but he loves still more something for which the others laugh at him. For he finds a whole fairy world for himself by watching the queer insects that abound in that countryside. He will stand in ecstasy before the splendor of a jeweled beetle or the wings of a butterfly. What fairies in the world could have such beautiful wings?

Now he is tramping back home to go to school in the town of St. Léons, in southern France where he was born.

A queer room that where Henri goes to school after this! It is at once a school, a kitchen, a bedroom, a dining-room,

*This tale of the French naturalist, Jean Henri Fabre (1823-1915), is told from autobiographical material in his own works *Souvenirs Entomologiques*, translated into English in *Insect Adventures*, *Animal Life in Field and Garden*, etc.

THROUGH FAIRY HALLS

a chicken house, and a piggery! On either side of the enormous fireplace are recesses in the wall. These recesses are beds, and each has two sliding doors to shut the sleeper in at night. Over in the sunny nook by the window stands the master's desk; on three-legged stools before the hearth, sit the scholars, and there, before them in an enormous cauldron over the flames, hangs the pigs' food simmering and giving off jets of steam with a puff-puff-puffing sound. Sometimes the boys take care to leave the schoolroom door open. Then the little porkers, attracted by the smell of food, come running in. They go trotting up to Henri, grunting and curling their tails, poking their cold, pink snouts into his hand in search of a scrap of bread. The master flicks his handkerchief—snick! Off go the little pigs! All to no use! A moment later, behold, in the doorway, old Madame Hen with her velvet-coated brood! The boys crumble pieces of bread and vie with each other to call the little chicks to them. It was not much Henri could learn in such a school. No! He held a book up in front of his face, but he never even learned his letters till his father brought home a book in which animals taught the alphabet—A is for Ass, and so on! Then Henri was overjoyed! Animals forever! Those beasts soon taught him his letters!

Plants and insects and animals—on every side what things of interest in the world! Up on the hill near the village, a miller had dammed up a brook to make a reservoir for his mill wheel. The reservoir was surrounded by a high, frowning wall all darkly bearded with ferns. But one day Henri hoisted himself on a playfellow's shoulders and peered over into the water. The water was covered with scum, slimy green scum like a carpet; and, in the gaps of that carpet, there lazily swam about a black and yellow reptile. Now it lay in wait, ugly, fierce, and still. Then a beautiful thing with shining wings flew innocently by. The reptile opened its jaws. Snap, it caught the creature! It devoured the shining thing. Hah! Here was the very dragon of Grandmother's fireside tales! In fancy, Henri saw it as one of those great monsters lurking and lying in wait to spring out on beautiful maidens. He jumped down in a hurry. He had seen a salamander.

And if he had found the dragon of Grandmother's fairy tales, he found in the insect world all the other characters and all the thrilling adventures Granny told about. Little worms, carrying tufts and feathers on their heads, were pygmy princes adorned with plumes. Beetles, with their hard wingcases, were little knights in armor.

186

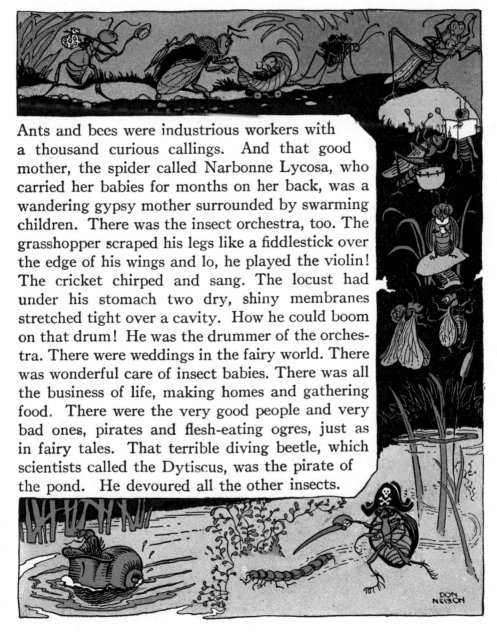

Ants and bees were industrious workers with a thousand curious callings. And that good mother, the spider called Narbonne Lycosa, who carried her babies for months on her back, was a wandering gypsy mother surrounded by swarming children. There was the insect orchestra, too. The grasshopper scraped his legs like a fiddlestick over the edge of his wings and lo, he played the violin! The cricket chirped and sang. The locust had under his stomach two dry, shiny membranes stretched tight over a cavity. How he could boom on that drum! He was the drummer of the orchestra. There were weddings in the fairy world. There was wonderful care of insect babies. There was all the business of life, making homes and gathering food. There were the very good people and very bad ones, pirates and flesh-eating ogres, just as in fairy tales. That terrible diving beetle, which scientists called the Dytiscus, was the pirate of the pond. He devoured all the other insects.

But there was one little creature who knew how to play a trick and escape the pirate beetle. That was the caddis worm, the grub of the caddis fly. The little caddis worm not only made its own clothes out of sticks and other material; it even made a traveling house out of an empty snail's shell. And when it was wrapped in sticks and protected in the shell, it floated around on the ponds hiding from pirate beetles. Those beetles lurked in the rocks, waiting to catch their prey, and when one of the terrible pirates spied the floating house which hid a caddis worm, he popped out and seized it fiercely, trying to rip it open by tearing off shells and sticks. But, while he was thus busy, the little caddis worm slipped out the door of its house, all unnoticed by the pirate. Looking like a small white sausage, it slipped between his legs, passed safely under his fangs and madly fled away. Then didn't the pirate look silly when he found how he had been tricked!

If that was an interesting story, here was another as good. There were slave-hunting Robbers in the insect world. These were the little red ants. They did not know how to bring up their children nor even how to get their own food; they had to have servants to keep house for them and feed them. So they made a practice of stealing children to wait on their community. When the hot weather of June and July set in, the red ants left their barracks and set out on a robbing expedition, their column five or six yards long. As soon as they approached an anthill, the front soldiers in the line halted and spread out their ranks while the others came up from the rear. Then scouts were sent out to examine the anthill. But they came back and reported that this was not the home of the kind of ant they wished to attack. So the column formed again. Off it marched in good order over mountains of dried leaves, through jungles of the grass. Hah! There at last was what they were looking for—a city of black ants! The red ants made a dash!

THROUGH FAIRY HALLS

They swarmed down to the dor- mitories where the black ant babies slept! There were all those babies wrapped neatly in swaddling clothes, that is, in their little cocoons. Each one of the red ants seized a swaddled baby and ran from the burrow with her booty! Then what a scrimmage there was at the gates of that underground city! The black ants defended their home, but the red ants attacked them savagely. In time the red ants won, then they raced off in a hurry, each bearing in her jaws her prize of a swaddled baby! In the city of the red ants, the black ant babies grew up. There they became willing slaves, keeping house industriously, gathering food for their masters, and minding the red ant babies.

Henri knew the story of Cinderella, too, how she sat among the cinders and longed to go to the ball. Then the fairy godmother arrived and under the fairy's wand a pumpkin became a fine coach; six mice turned into horses; a rat became a coachman; six lizards were liveried footmen; and Cinderella's shabby clothes were changed into splendid garments, gleaming with gold and silver. But what was magic like that compared to the magic that could be performed by that great fairy, Nature? There went a miserable little caterpillar, crawling humbly along, or maybe an ugly worm. One wave of the wand from the fairy, Nature, and those miserable little creatures went to sleep in cocoons. A miracle occurred! They were all transformed! Out came the worm, a beetle, shining with gold and jewels! Out came the caterpillar, a glorious butterfly whose wings outshone Cinderella's finest garments.

When Henri Fabre grew up, he continued to study the ways of insects in his little pink house with green shutters at Serignan, in France. There his garden was a riot of verdure, and the sweet air was always full of the music of insects' hummings. There those little creatures each told the student its secret and its history.

How he loved them all, how tenderly he wrote of them, how accurately he observed them! Other scientists dissected insects and sought the secret of their life from death; Fabre observed his alive and sought the secret of their life from the marvelous instinct that directed all their ways. With reverence and awe he stood before the unerring Power that guides the wild bee and the wasp, though they may be carried miles away from home, back over vast and unknown spaces, surely to their nests. How wonderfully those little creatures built their nests, how certain was the power that guided them, how surely each fulfilled his given task! Studying in his sunny garden, Fabre not only loved insects, but he also taught others to love them.

It was Henri Fabre who first learned that every living creature, even an insect, has an interesting life of its own. And to him the best fairy book ever written could be read by simply overturning a stone and seeing all the wonders of life that had been going on beneath it. Thus Henri discovered the Fairyland of Science and revealed it to the world.

FAIRY FORESTS*
ALFRED NOYES

I WONDER if you've ever dreamed,
  In summer's noonday sleep,
Of what the thyme and heather seemed
  To ladybirds that creep
Like little, crimson, shimmering gems
Between the tiny, twisted stems
  Of fairy forests deep;
And what it looks like as they pass
Through jungles of the golden grass.

*From *Collected Poems*, published by Frederick A. Stokes Company.

190

Pigling and Her Proud Sister*

A Korean Cinderella Tale

WILLIAM ELLIOT GRIFFIS

Pear Blossom had been the name of a little Korean maid who was suddenly left motherless. When her father, Kang Wa, who was a magistrate high in office, married again, he took for his wife a proud widow whose daughter, born to Kang Wa, was named Violet. Mother and daughter hated housework and made Pear Blossom clean the rice, cook the food and attend the fire in the kitchen. They were hateful in their treatment of Pear Blossom, and, besides never speaking a kind word, called her Pigling, or Little Pig, which made the girl weep often.

*Taken from *Unmannerly Tiger and Other Korean Tales* published by Thomas Y. Crowell Company.

It did no good to complain to her father, for he was always busy. He smoked his yard-long pipe and played checkers hour by hour, apparently caring more about having his great white coat properly starched and lustred than for his daughter to be happy. His linen had to be beaten with a laundry club until it glistened like hoar frost.

Poor Pigling had to perform this task of washing, starching and glossing, in addition to the kitchen work, and the rat-tat-tat of her laundry stick was often heard in the outer room till after midnight, when the heartless mother and daughter had long been asleep.

There was to be a great festival in the city and for many days preparations were made in the house to get the father ready in his best robe and hat, and the women in their finery, to go out and see the king and the royal procession.

Poor Pigling wanted very much to have a look at the pageant but the mother, setting before her a huge straw bag of unhulled rice and a big cracked water jar, told her she must husk all the rice, draw water from the well, and fill the crock to the brim before she dared to go out on the street.

What a task to hull with her fingers three bushels of rice and fill up a leaky vessel! Pigling wept bitterly.

While she was brooding thus and opening the straw bag to begin spreading the rice out on mats, she heard a whir and rush of wings and down came a flock of pigeons. They first lighted on her head and shoulders, and then hopping to the floor began diligently to work with beak and claw, and in a few minutes the rice lay in a heap, clean, white and glistening, while with their pink toes they pulled away the hulls and put these in a separate pile. Then, after a great chattering and cooing, the flock was off and away.

Pigling was so amazed at this wonderful work of the birds

that she scarcely knew how to be thankful enough. But, alas, there was still the cracked crock to be filled. Just as she took hold of the bucket to begin, there crawled out of the fire hole a sooty, black imp, named Tokgabi.

"Don't cry," he squeaked out. "I'll mend the broken part and fill the big jar for you." Forthwith, he stopped up the crack with clay, and pouring a dozen buckets of water from the well into the crock, filled it to brimming so the water spilled over on all sides. Then Tokgabi bowed and crawled into the flues again, before the astonished girl could thank her helper.

So Pigling had time to dress in her plain but clean clothes. She went off and saw the royal banners and the king's grand procession of thousands of loyal men.

The next time, Violet and her mother planned a picnic on the mountain. So the refreshments were prepared and Pigling had to work hard in starching the dresses to be worn—jackets, long skirts, belts, sashes, and what not, until she nearly dropped with fatigue. Yet instead of thanking and cheering her, the heart-

less woman told Pigling she must not go out until she had hoed all the weeds in the garden and pulled up all the grass between the stones of the walk.

Again the poor girl's face was wet with tears. She was left at home alone, while the others went off in fine clothes, with plenty to eat and drink, for a day of merrymaking.

While she wept thus, a huge, black cow came along and out of its great, liquid eyes seemed to beam compassion upon the kitchen slave. Then, in ten mouthfuls, the animal ate up the weeds, and, between its hoof and lips, soon made an end of the grass in the stone pathway.

With her tears dried, Pigling followed this wonderful brute out over the meadows into the woods, where she found the most delicious fruit her eyes ever rested upon. She tasted and enjoyed, feasting to the full and then returned home.

When Violet heard of the astonishing doings of the black cow, she determined to enjoy a feast in the forest also. So on the next gala-day she stayed home and let the kitchen drudge go to see the royal parade. Pigling could not understand why she was excused, even for a few hours, from the pots and kettles, but she was still more surprised by the gift from her stepmother of a rope of cash to spend for dainties. Gratefully thanking the woman, she put on her best clothes and was soon on the main street of the city enjoying the gay sights and looking at the happy people. There were tight rope dancing, music with drum and flute by bands of strolling players, tricks by conjurers and mountebanks, with mimicking and castanets, posturing by the singing girls and fun of all sorts. Boys peddling honey candy, barley sugar and sweetmeats were out by the dozen. At the eating-house, Pigling had a good dinner of fried fish, boiled rice with red peppers, turnips, dried persimmons, roasted chestnuts and candied orange, and felt as happy as a queen.

THROUGH FAIRY HALLS

The selfish Violet had stayed home, not to relieve Pigling of work, but to see the wonderful cow. So, when the black animal appeared and found its friend gone, it went off into the forest. Violet at once followed in the tracks of the cow that took it into its head to go very fast, and into unpleasant places. Soon the girl found herself in a swamp, wet, miry and full of brambles. Still hoping for wonderful fruit, she kept on until she was tired out and the cow was no longer to be seen. Then, muddy and bedraggled, she tried to go back, but the thorny bushes tore her clothes, spoiled her hands and so scratched her face that when at last, she got home, she was in rags and her beauty gone.

But Pigling, rosy and round, looked so lovely that a young man from the south, who saw her that day, was struck by her beauty. As he wanted a wife, he immediately sought to find out where she lived. Then he secured a go-between who visited both families and made all arrangements for the betrothal and marriage.

Grand was the wedding. The groom, Su-Wen, was dressed in white and black silk robes, with a rich horsehair cap and head-dress denoting his rank as a gentleman.

Charming, indeed, looked Pear Blossom, in her robe of bro-cade. Dainty were her red kid shoes curved upward at the toes.

So with her original name now restored, and henceforth called Ewa, or Pear Blossom, the daughter of Kang Wa was to be Mrs. Su-Wen.

Leaving her home in a palanquin borne by four lusty bearers, Pear Blossom went forth to live amid rich rice fields of a south-ern province. Her home was with a father and mother-in-law, who, having no other children but their one son, became very fond of their new daughter. Summer after summer the pear trees bloomed and Ewa, the Pear Blossom, lived ever happily.

MY BOOK HOUSE

LITTLE PICTURES FROM FAR JAPAN

SNOW
The snow fell in the night,
And people rouse each other up
To see the lovely sight.
—*Ransetsu* (1654-1707)

OFF WE'LL GO
Off we'll go
To see the snow,
Till we take a tumble!
Basho (1643-1694)

In Japan, everyone writes verses—farm girls in the rice fields, fishermen fishing at night, porters, children, grown-ups. They write verses on screens, on cups and plates, on painted fans, anywhere, in fact. They even hold poetry picnics where everyone must write a poem. Nowhere is poetry more dearly loved than in Japan.

THROUGH FAIRY HALLS

WILLOWS IN THE SNOW
The willows hanging low,
Shake from their long and
    trailing skirts
The freshly fallen snow.
            —*Tsuru*

SNOW BLOSSOMS
When the snow falls,
Behold each bush and tree,
    Till then fast bound by
        winter,
Breaks forth into such blos-
    soms
As in spring we never see.

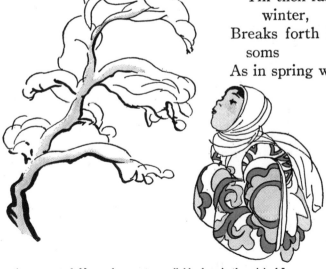

These tiny verses or *hokkus*, only seventeen syllables long in the original Japanese, are typical of Japan. Japanese poets love all the beauty of the world—willows in the snow; the moon; the winds; the birds; their delicate blossoming fruit trees, so beautiful in the spring; crickets; frogs; butterflies; everything that has life.

The Fisherman Who Caught the Sun

A Hawaiian Legend

FAR across the blue Pacific Ocean, on the mountainous little island of Hawaii, a brown Hawaiian mother sat before a tiny straw-thatched hut, and told her little brown children stories. Before her the great round sun was sinking toward the ocean. Out on the water were big brown boys in their queer shaped canoes; others were swimming about, and some were riding the waves, standing up straight and balancing in a wonderful fashion on narrow boards that were carried landwards, rocking, and rolling, on the curling crests of the waves.

The younger children were all at home and grouped about their mother. They had decked themselves out gaily with garlands of flowers and long strings of colored seeds as they dearly loved to do, and, while they watched the setting sun, their mother told them, in the soft, musical Hawaiian tongue, an old Hawaiian tale:

"Many, many years ago, the Sun used to burst forth from the ocean at dawn and race so swiftly across the sky, that he would fling himself over the top of the great fire mountain and sink down again into the ocean before half a day's work was done. Sunset followed so quickly on sunrise that men began to complain:

" 'Alas! The Sun, in his headlong haste, is cheating us of our due. We have not daylight enough to finish our hunting and fishing, to build our canoes, and gather our yams and bananas and cocoanuts. Night comes on and finds our work but half done.'

"Then there rose up a brave Fisherman and he said: 'I shall go to the Sun and teach him to make his journey as he should. He shall no more bolt across the sky at any pace he may choose.'

"The Fisherman's friends began to wail, and bid him remember what it meant to face such a powerful foe as the Sun. But the Fisherman never once stopped plaiting long ropes to make

In Hawaii, each event in life has its music celebrated by the native instrument, the ukulele, with its weird harmonies and slurring effects. *Aloha* is the song of farewell. *Kuu Home* sings the joy of plantation life.

a snare, and he said: 'I do not fear the Sun. In this snare I shall catch him.'

"So when the Sun had run his mad race for the day and left the world to night, the Fisherman got into his canoe and sailed out into the Eastern ocean. Far he sailed and farther through the shadows, down the silvery path that the moon lit up across the dark waste of the waters. Thus he came to the very edge of the earth, to the spot where the Sun would soon burst forth when he rose from under the ocean. And there he set his snare, gripping tight in his hands the ends of the rope from which he had made it.

"Soon the moon set and the world was wrapped in darkness. Then the Fisherman sat in his rocking canoe on the edge of the world and waited. At last the darkness faded into gray; bright jewels of light flashed now and again from the ocean. Purple and rose appeared in the sky and lo! a small rim of the sun peeped up to touch the white crests of the waves into fire and set all the ocean aflame.

"Still the Fisherman sat in his rocking canoe on the edge of the world and waited. In another moment a flood of gold streamed over the earth and the whole great Sun burst forth to begin his wild race across the sky. But ah! he had bolted straight into the snare and was tangled close in its meshes. Then the Fisherman rose in his canoe, and pulled tight the ropes in his hand. The great Sun raged! He flared and flamed, but the Fisherman held on fast.

" 'Sun,' he cried, undaunted, 'from this day forth, you shall travel at proper speed. You shall no more do as you please and race at your own headlong pace across the sky. You shall give man a day that is long enough so he may finish his hunting and fishing, build his canoes and gather his yams and bananas and cocoanuts.'

"The rage of the Sun grew scorching, withering, blasting. He struggled with all his might to be free. But the Fisherman braced his feet, balanced his rocking canoe on the waves, and held to the ropes with a grip that would never, never yield. At last the Sun saw he had met his master. Then he slowly softened his glare and stood still.

" 'I promise,' he said, 'I will race no more at my own headlong pace, but will travel at proper speed, slowly, steadily, over the sky.'

"When he had promised thus, the Fisherman set him free, but he did not remove from him all of the ropes. Some he left fastened securely at the edge of the world in order to bind the Sun to keep his promise.

" 'You shall never again be free to have your own will,' he said.

"Then the Fisherman went back home and his people hailed him with music and singing, as one who had been their savior, for ever thereafter the Sun kept his word and the days were sufficiently long for all the work that had need to be done.

"But to this very day when the Sun rises or when he sets, you may still see the ropes hanging down. Look now, as he sinks toward the ocean! You say he is drawing water, but I tell you those brilliant rays that seem to anchor him to the sea, are in truth the meshes of that snare by which the Fisherman bound him."

DONN P. CRANE

THROUGH FAIRY HALLS

A TROPICAL MORNING AT SEA*

EDWARD ROWLAND SILL

OFF to the East the steady sun-track
  Golden meshes fill—
Webs of fire, that lace and tangle,
  Never a moment still.

Thinned to amber, rimmed with silver,
  Clouds in the distance dwell,
Clouds that are cool, for all their color,
  Pure as a rose-lipped shell.

HERBERT
RUDEEN

*Taken from *Hermitage and Later Poems*. Used by permission of, and special arrangement with, Houghton Mifflin Co., the publishers.

Aruman, a Hero of Java

ON THE island of Java, there once lived long ago, a boy
called Aruman. Now Aruman's mother was dead. It was
his good old nurse, Sumarr, who had brought him up. When he
was a baby, Sumarr wreathed his little brown body with jessamine
flowers; she made him toy umbrellas of white tanjong blossoms;
she played with him and loved him as tenderly as a mother.

But, one day, while Aruman was still a lad, there was much
noise of many people stirring in his father's house, and, toward
evening, a grand procession came up to the door. There were
men on hobby horses beating strange musical instruments; women
with paper birds, flowers, and tall fans of peacock feathers; all
accompanying a litter in which rode three flower-wreathed maidens.
Last of all, on horseback came Drahman, Aruman's father.

"It is a wedding procession, Sumarr! What does it mean?"
asked Aruman.

"Ah, little cricket," answered the nurse, "it means that thy
father has brought thee home a new mother. Up there she sits
in the litter with her maids. Ma Qualoan is her name."

Now Ma Qualoan had not long taken her place in Drahman's
household before she began to show a great dislike for Aruman.

THROUGH FAIRY HALLS

"'Tis a lazy lad of thine," she would say to Drahman. "All day long he does nothing but eat and sleep. Fie for shame!"

So Ma Qualoan went on till Aruman was shut out of his father's heart altogether. Aruman must live with the servants, Aruman must eat scraps from his father's table! And, when Aruman did at last make his way to Drahman, throw himself at his feet and beg that his love should return, Drahman drove the boy with harsh words out of his presence.

Sumarr did what she could to comfort the lad; but at last, from all Ma Qualoan said, Drahman grew fearful lest Aruman should do some deed so wicked as to bring shame upon him, so he determined to rid himself of the boy.

One day Aruman wandered alone into the forest. A shower of white blossoms floated down from the tanjong branches; red-and-orange flowers dropped from the flame-of-the-forest and lay like red embers on his path, but Aruman, who loved the flowers so well, had no eyes for them today. He was thinking only how he had been shut out from his father's heart. So he sat himself down beneath the spreading branches of a giant waringin tree near a stream and wept. Soon, as he sat there, lo, he saw his father come toward him! Aruman rose in respectful greeting, but Drahman stood sternly still, pointing one finger toward the mass of small trunks that formed the giant trunk of the waringin tree.

"Like the waringin tree, I hoped my sons would be," said Drahman, "countless in number, sturdy, upright and all joined as one to mine honor. But lo, I have only thee who disgrace me!" So saying, he seized Aruman, bound him with ropes, and cast him into the river.

"Father! Father!" shrieked the boy, but the stream bore him on and away.

203

Presently, as he floated along, he came upon an alligator and a fish who were lurking in the river. "Ah," he cried to the two, "swallow me up, for who is there left in the world to care?"

But the alligator and the fish, after a single glance at the lad, cried: "Swallow such an one as you? Nay! That will we never do! You are destined to do great deeds! We will not swallow, but help you." So they guided him in safety to the bank of the stream and there loosed him from the cords by which he was bound.

"Stay a moment," said the alligator. "I have that in my keeping which has long waited for just such a lad as you." He vanished and soon reappeared with a pair of magic shoes.

"With these," said he, as Aruman bound them on his feet, "you can walk on the water as easily as on dry land."

So Aruman thanked the alligator and the fish for their kindness and stepped out confidently on the water. Making his way down the river, he walked as far as the ocean. And when he saw the boundless blue sea stretching off before him, he must even venture out on that. As he wandered along far from land enjoying his new accomplishment, he presently saw a vessel. At the same time he, himself, was observed by the Captain of the ship, who seeing a boy walking on the surface of the water, could scarcely believe his eyes. As Aruman drew nearer, however, the Captain invited him aboard and ordered him to be served with the sailors' usual repast, which consisted of rice and salt fish.

THROUGH FAIRY HALLS

During the meal, the boy recounted his adventures and sorrows to the Captain and the crew; but the Captain had noted the magic shoes which Aruman was wearing and at once began to think how he could get them for himself.

"What use are those shoes to you, boy?" said he. "Mark my words, some day when you feel the safest, you'll sink. Give them to me and I will give you my flying cloak. In that, you can skim over the water like a swallow or soar up into the clouds!"

"Very well," said the boy, "give me the cloak for my shoes."

Now the cloak had indeed been given to the Captain as a flying cloak; but, though he had often wrapped it about him and tried timidly and cautiously to fly, he had never been able to lift himself off the ground. So he had concluded the garment was useless and was more than willing to trade it. Yet the moment that Aruman stepped confidently forth in it with never a doubt that he could do just what the Captain said, he darted up through the air and soared like a strong-winged bird.

"Now who would have thought it?" mumbled the Captain. Then he, himself, started out wearing the magic shoes. Uncertainly he walked till a panic of fear overwhelmed him and he began to sink. The shoes would not bear him up the moment he was afraid. Only because he was an expert swimmer, was he able to regain his boat. Very much vexed he cried out, "Cheat! Rogue! You have robbed me of my wonderful cloak! These shoes of yours are worthless!"

Aruman laughed good-naturedly as he hovered about overhead but the Captain went ashore in a small boat and challenged the boy to fight. So Aruman descended to the ground, still without any anger, for he hoped to appease the Captain by speaking courteous words. But the Captain was now so beside himself that he would not listen to reason.

"Come on! Come on!" he cried. "I'll soon do for you, you wretch!" And he drew his kriss, and flourished it, and rushed furiously upon the lad. But Aruman, though young, could not be aroused to anger. He fought with such coolness and courage, he soon had the wrathful Captain entirely at his mercy. When the man had been brought to his knees and forced to acknowledge that he alone was to blame for the bargain they had made, Aruman flew off, heading toward his father's dwelling.

He passed over valleys and forests, until he came at last into a strange, gloomy country. Under the sombre branches of gigantic trees, numberless caverns yawned. Wondering what could be within such bottomless pits, Aruman looked into one. The mouth of it was so black that it seemed to be the entrance to a region of endless night. But, while he stood gazing into it, a figure suddenly appeared, lighting up the recess with a weird, red light. As it drew near the lad, the figure seemed to be that of a wrinkled old woman, bearing a queer, ill-favored, black bird in one bony hand. Mumbling some strange words, she let the bird fly away. Up into the air it mounted, circling around overhead. And ever and anon it took the form of a man with the face of one in deep sorrow for some evil deed he had done.

THROUGH FAIRY HALLS

Before these strange apparitions, the boy stood his ground as firmly as he had before the Captain. Then the weird woman began throwing pebbles on the ground. They turned into little headless dwarfs that danced and swarmed about, but Aruman extended his arm with a gesture of command and the grotesque phantoms vanished. Then there appeared in their place a maiden lovely as dawn, wreathed in flowers and smiling on him. Her, Aruman would gladly have kept before his eyes; but, in another moment, she, too, had faded away and he was left alone.

Slowly he turned to grope his way out of the darkness. His foot slipped on the marshy ground, he stumbled over rocks and stones. But, though he knew it not, the woman he had thought a witch, was a good fairy, watching over him. Having satisfied herself that he was a brave and dauntless boy, she despatched two tigers to walk on either side of him, and, by the light of their eyes, which shone like lamps, he was guided out of the jungle.

Aruman now made straight for his father's home; and, when he was come as far as the great waringin tree when his father had cast him into the stream, he saw Drahman himself standing on the spot where he had committed his wicked deed. For the first time anger surged up in Aruman's heart. He drew his kriss to strike him; but, as his father turned his face toward him, lo, there was in his features the same expression of sorrow and regret for

what he had done that the strange, black bird had revealed to Aruman in the shadowy land of phantoms. Slowly Aruman dropped his kriss. "Ah!" he cried. "If that is how thou art punished in thine own heart, then go and wash thy heart clean in the waters of Zem-Zem. Aruman forgives thee."

"I go, my son!" cried Drahman and fled from Aruman's presence.

Aruman then went on home, where he found Ma Qualoan in the portico, counting over the jewels which Drahman had showered upon her. The boy was tempted again! Just to fall on her with his kriss! But, recalling once again the strange vision of the bird, he did no more than show himself suddenly before her. Seeing him, whom she had wronged, thus returned so unexpectedly, Ma Qualoan fell prostrate before him. He passed her without a word and went on to find the good Sumarr.

That night some unseen force bore Ma Qualoan into the forest. There she was chained to a rock overlooking a pool wherein she saw clearly reflected all her own wicked deeds.

For some time Aruman lived on quietly in his home attended by the faithful Sumarr. But the news of his exploits reached

the ears of the King of Java, who invited the daring youth to come and live in his palace. There, to his great astonishment, Aruman again beheld the lovely maiden of his vision in the forest. She was the daughter of the King and, in time, she became his bride. Some years later, Aruman himself became the King and to this day, he is a favorite hero with the people of Java who often recount his adventures in little puppet shows.

*The Javanese love to see their old tales like *Aruman* in shadow shows. Puppets or *wayangs* are shown behind a white-cloth screen while a man behind the screen tells the story of the play.

THROUGH FAIRY HALLS

A SONG FROM "THE FLOWER OF OLD JAPAN"*

ALFRED NOYES

There when the sunset colours the streets
    Everyone buys at wonderful stalls
Toys and chocolates, guns and sweets,
    Ivory pistols, and Persian shawls;
Everyone's pockets are crammed with gold;
    Nobody ever grows tired and old,
    And nobody calls you "Baby" there.

There with a hat like a round, white dish
    Upside down on each pig-tailed head,
Jugglers offer you snakes and fish,
    Dreams and dragons and gingerbread;
Beautiful books with marvellous pictures,
    Painted pirates and streaming gore,
And everyone reads, without any strictures,
    Tales he remembers for evermore.

*From *Collected Poems.* Reprinted by permission of Frederick A. Stokes Company.

The Moon-Maiden
A Japanese Fairy Tale

There dwelt once on the edge of the forest at the foot of Fujiyama, a bamboo-cutter and his wife. They were honest, industrious people who loved each other dearly, but no children had come to bless them, and therefore they were not happy.

"Ah, husband," mourned the wife, "more welcome to me than cherry blossoms in springtime would be a little child of my own."

One evening she stood on the porch of her flimsy bamboo cottage and lifted her eyes toward the everlasting snows on the top of Fujiyama. Then, with swelling breast, she bowed herself to the ground and cried out to the Honorable Mountain:

"Fuji no yama, I am sad because no little head lies on my breast, no childish laughter gladdens our home. Send me, I pray thee, from thine eternal purity, a little one to comfort me."

As she spoke, lo! from the top of the Honorable Mountain

210

there suddenly sparkled a gleam of light as when the face of a child is lit by a beaming smile.

"Husband, husband, come quickly," cried the good woman. "See there on the heights of Fujiyama a child is beaming upon me."

"It is but your fancy," said the bamboo-cutter and yet he added, "I will climb up and see what is there."

So he followed the trail of silvery light through the forest, and up the steep slope where Fujiyama towered white and still above him. At last he stopped below a tall bamboo by the bank of a mountain stream, from whence the glow seemed to come. There, cradled in the branches of the tree, he found a tiny moon-child, fragile, dainty, radiant, clad in flimsy, filmy moon-shine, more beautiful than anything he had ever seen before.

"Ah, little shining creature, who are you?" he cried.

"I am the Princess Moonbeam," answered the child. "The Moon Lady is my mother, but she has sent me to earth to comfort the sad heart of your wife."

"Then, little Princess," said the Woodman eagerly, "I will take you home to be our child."

So the woodman bore her carefully down the mountain side.

"See, wife," he called, "what the Moon Lady has sent you."

Then was the good woman overjoyed. She took the little moon-child and held her close, and the moon-child's little arms went twining about her neck, as she nestled snug against her breast. So was the good wife's longing satisfied at last.

As the years passed by, Princess Moonbeam brought nothing but joy to the woodman and his wife. Lovelier and lovelier she grew. Fair was her face and radiant, her eyes were shining stars, and her hair had the gleam of a misty silver halo. About her, too, there was a strange, unearthly charm that made all who saw her love her.

One day there came riding by in state the Mikado himself.

He saw how the Princess Moonbeam lit up the humble cottage, and he loved her. Then the Mikado would have taken her back with him to court, but no!—the longing of the earthly father and mother for a little child had been fulfilled, the Princess Moonbeam had stayed with them till she was a maiden grown, and now the time had come when she must go back to her sky mother, the Lady in the Moon.

"Stay, stay with me on earth!" cried the Mikado.

"Stay, stay with us on earth!" cried the bamboo-cutter and his wife. Then the Mikado got two thousand archers and set them on guard close about the house and even on the roof, that none might get through to take her. But when the moon rose white and full, a line of light like a silver bridge sprung arching down from heaven to earth and floating along that gleaming path came the Lady from the Moon. The Mikado's soldiers stood as though turned to stone. Straight through their midst the Moon Lady passed and bent caressingly down for her long-absent child. She wrapped her close in a garment of silver mist. Then she caught her tenderly in her arms, and led her gently back to the sky. The Princess Moonbeam was glad to go back home, yet as she went, she wept silvery tears for those she was leaving behind. And lo! her bright, shining tears took wings and floated away to carry a message of love, that should comfort the Mikado, and her earthly father and mother.

To this very day the gleaming tears of the little Princess Moonbeam are seen to float hither and yon about the marshes and groves of Japan. The children chase them with happy cries and say, "See the fire-flies! How beautiful they are!" Then their mothers, in the shadow of Fujiyama, tell the children this legend— how the fire-flies are shining love messages of the little Princess Moonbeam, flitting down to bring comfort to earth from her far-off home in the silver moon.

THROUGH FAIRY HALLS

Little Nell and Mrs. Jarley's Wax-Work[*]

CHARLES DICKENS

IT WAS not a shabby, dingy, dusty cart, but a smart little house upon wheels, with white dimity curtains festooning the windows, and window shutters of blue picked out with panels of orange. Neither was it a gipsy caravan, for at the open door (graced with a bright brass knocker) sat a lady, stout and comfortable to look upon, her bonnet trembling with bows. And this lady's occupation was the very pleasant one of taking tea. The tea things, including a cold knuckle of ham, were set forth upon a drum, covered with a white napkin; and there, as if at the most convenient roundtable in all the world, sat this roving lady.

It happened that at that moment she had her cup to her lips, and it was not until she was in the act of setting it down, that she beheld an old man and a little girl walking slowly by, and glancing at her tea things with longing eyes.

"Hey," cried the lady of the caravan shortly but kindly, "who are you?"

The little girl, who was pretty, and blue-eyed, answered in a soft voice, "My name is Nell." Then she took the hand of the old man with a tender, protecting air, as though he were the child and she his mother, "and this is my grandfather. Can you tell us how far we shall have to walk to the next town?"

The stout lady answered that the town was at least eight miles off.

This information a little discouraged the child, who could scarcely keep back a tear as she glanced along the darkening road. Her grandfather made no complaint, but he sighed heavily as he leaned upon his staff, and vainly tried to see into the dusty distance.

The lady of the caravan was about to gather her tea things together and clean the table, but noting the child's anxious man-

*Arranged from *The Old Curiosity Shop*.

ner, she hesitated and stopped. The little girl curtsied, thanked her for her information, and had already led the old man some fifty yards or so away, when the lady of the caravan called to her to return.

"Come nearer, nearer still," said she, beckoning to her to ascend the steps. "Are you hungry, child?"

"Not very, but we are tired, and it's—it is a long way."

"Is your home in the next town?"

"No, we have no home! We are wanderers."

"Well, hungry or not, you had better have some tea. I suppose you are agreeable to that, old gentleman?"

The grandfather humbly pulled off his hat and thanked her. The lady of the caravan then bade him come up the steps likewise, but the drum proving too small a table for two, they went down again, and sat upon the grass, where she handed them the tea-tray, the bread and butter, the knuckle of ham, and in short everything of which she had eaten herself.

"Set 'em out near the hind wheels, child, that's the best place," she said, directing the arrangements from above. "Now hand up the teapot for a little more hot water, and a pinch of fresh tea, and then both of you eat and drink as much as you can, and don't spare anything; that's all I ask of you."

So the two made a hearty meal and enjoyed it to the utmost.

While they were thus engaged, the lady of the caravan alighted on the earth, and with her hands clasped behind her, and her large bonnet trembling excessively, walked up and down in a very stately manner, looking over the caravan from time to time with an air of calm delight, and enjoying particularly the orange panels and the brass knocker, of which she was very proud.

When she had taken this gentle exercise for some time, she sat down upon the steps and called "George"; whereupon a man in a carter's frock, who had been hidden from sight in a hedge, parted the twigs that concealed him and appeared in a sitting

attitude, supporting on his legs a baking-dish, and
bearing in his right hand a knife, and in his left a fork.

"Yes, Missus," said George.

"How did you find the cold pie, George?"

"It warn't amiss, mum."

"We are not a heavy load, George. Would these two travelers make much difference to the horses, if we took them with us?" asked his mistress, pointing to Nell and the old man who were painfully preparing to resume their journey on foot.

"They'd make a difference in course," said George doggedly.

But his mistress turned to the old man and the child and told them they should go on to the town with her in the caravan. Nell was overjoyed and thanked the lady earnestly.

She helped with great readiness to put away the tea things; and, the horses being by that time harnessed, she mounted into the vehicle, followed by her delighted grandfather. The lady then shut the door and sat herself down by her drum at an open window. The steps were taken down by George and stowed under the carriage. Then away they went, with a great noise of flapping and creaking and straining; and the bright brass knocker, which nobody ever knocked at, knocking one perpetual double knock of its own accord as they jolted along.

When they had traveled slowly forward for some short distance, Nell ventured to look round the caravan and observe it more closely. One-half of it was carpeted, and so partitioned off at the further end as to form a sleeping-place, made after the fashion of a berth on board ship. This was shaded, like the little windows, with fair white curtains, and looked comfortable enough, though by what kind of gymnastic exercise the lady of the caravan ever managed to get into it, was a mystery. The other half served for a kitchen, and was fitted up with a stove, whose small chimney passed through the roof. It held also, a closet or larder, several chests, a great pitcher of water, and a few cooking-utensils. These latter necessaries hung upon the walls, which were also ornamented with a triangle and a couple of well-thumbed tambourines.

The lady of the caravan sat at one window, and little Nell and her grandfather at the other, while the caravan jogged on.

THROUGH FAIRY HALLS

At first the two travelers spoke little, and only in whispers but, as they grew more familiar with the place, they ventured to talk about the country through which they were passing, and the different objects that presented themselves, until the old man fell asleep. The lady of the caravan, seeing this, invited Nell to come and sit beside her.

"Well, child," she said, "how do you like this way of traveling?"

Nell replied that she thought it was very pleasant indeed.

Then getting up, the lady brought out from a corner a large roll of canvas about a yard in width, which she laid upon the floor and spread open with her foot, until it nearly reached from one end of the caravan to the other. "There, child," she said proudly, "read that." Nell walked down it, and read aloud the inscription, which was written in enormous black letters,

> ## JARLEY'S WAX-WORK

"Read it again," said the lady, enjoying the fine-sounding words.

"Jarley's Wax-Work," repeated Nell.

"That's me," said the lady. I am Mrs. Jarley."

And she unfolded another scroll, whereon was written,

> ## ONE-HUNDRED FIGURES THE FULL SIZE OF LIFE
> ## THE ONLY STUPENDOUS COLLECTION
> ## OF REAL WAX-WORK IN THE WORLD!

"I never saw any wax-work, ma'am," said Nell. "Is it funnier than Punch?"

"Funnier!" said Mrs. Jarley, in a shrill voice. "It is not funny at all. It's figures of people made out of wax, and so like life, that if wax-work only spoke and walked about, you'd hardly know the difference." And with great dignity she showed a

217

"NOW BEING SHOWN WITHIN" "THE GENUINE AND ONLY JARLEY"

If I knowed a donkey wot wouldn't go
To see Mrs. Jarley's wax-work show,
Do you think I'd acknowledge him?
Oh - No - No -
Then run to JARLEY'S

colored handbill advertising her show.

"Is it here in the cart, ma'am?" asked Nell.

"Is what here, child?"

"The wax-work, ma'am."

"Why bless you, child, what are you thinking of—how could such a collection be here, where you see everything except the inside of one little cupboard and a few boxes? It's gone on in the other vans to the Assembly-rooms, and there it'll be exhibited the day after to-morrow. You are going to the same town, and you'll see it I dare say."

"I shall not be in the town, I think, ma'am," said the child.

"Not there!" cried Mrs. Jarley. "Then where will you be?"

"I—I—don't quite know. I am not certain."

"You don't mean to say that you're traveling about the country without knowing where you're going to?" said the lady of the caravan. "What curious people you are!"

"We are poor people, ma'am," returned Nell, "and are only wandering about. We have nothing to do; I wish we had."

"You amaze me more and more," said Mrs. Jarley, after remaining for some time as silent as one of her own figures.

At length she summoned the driver to come under the window at which she was seated, and held a long conversation with him in a low tone, as if she were asking his advice on an important point. Then she drew in her head again, and, seeing the grandfather had awakened, said:

"Do you want a good place for your granddaughter to work, master? If you do, I can put her in the way of getting one."

THROUGH FAIRY HALLS

"I can't leave her," answered the old man. "We can't separate. What would become of me without her?"

"If you want to employ yourself, too," said Mrs. Jarley, "there would be plenty for you to do in the way of helping to dust the figures, and so forth. What I want your granddaughter for, is to point out to the company; she would soon learn who the figures are, and she has a way with her that people wouldn't think unpleasant, though she does come after me; for I've been always accustomed to go round with visitors myself. It's not a common offer, bear in mind," said the lady, rising into the grand tone in which she was accustomed to address her audiences, "it's Jarley's wax-work, remember."

As to salary she could pledge herself to no certain sum until she had seen what Nell could do, and watched her in the performance of her duties. But board and lodging, both for her and her grandfather, she bound herself to provide, and she furthermore passed her word that the board should always be good.

Nell and her grandfather consulted together, while Mrs. Jarley, with her hands behind her, walked up and down the caravan with uncommon dignity.

"Now, child," cried Mrs. Jarley, coming to a halt as Nell turned toward her.

"We are very much obliged to you, ma'am," said Nell, "and thankfully accept your offer."

"And you'll never be sorry for it," returned Mrs. Jarley. "I'm pretty sure of that. So as that's all settled, let us have a bit of supper."

In the meanwhile, the caravan came at last upon the paved streets of a town which were clear of passengers, and quiet, for it was by this time near midnight and the townspeople were all abed. As it was too late an hour to go to the room where they were to show the wax-work, they turned aside into a piece of waste ground that lay just within the old town gate, and drew up there for the night, near to another caravan, which was employed in carrying the wonderful figures from place to place.

This caravan being empty (for it had left the wax-work at the place of exhibition) was pointed out to the old man as his sleeping-place for the night; and within its wooden walls Nell made him up the best bed she could from the materials at hand. For herself, she was to sleep in Mrs. Jarley's own traveling-carriage, as a mark of that lady's favor and confidence.

Sleep hung upon the eyelids of the child so long, that, when she awoke, Mrs. Jarley was already decorated with her large bonnet, and actively engaged in preparing breakfast. She received Nell's apology for being so late, with perfect good-humor, and said that she would not have roused her if she had slept on until noon. The meal finished, Nell assisted to wash the cups and saucers, and put them in their proper places. These household duties performed, Mrs. Jarley arrayed herself in an exceedingly bright shawl for the purpose of making a very grand appearance as she walked through the streets of the town.

"The van will come on after me to bring the boxes," said Mrs. Jarley, "and you had better come in it, child. I am obliged to walk, very much against my will; but the people expect it of me. They must have a look at Mrs. Jarley, owner of the one and only Jarley's Wax-Work. How do I look, child?"

Nell returned a satisfactory reply, and Mrs. Jarley, after sticking a great many pins into various parts of her figure, and trying several times to see her own back, was at last satisfied with her appearance, and went forth majestically.

The caravan followed at no great distance. As it went jolting through the streets, Nell peeped from the window, curious to see in what kind of place they were. It was a pretty town, with a square, in the middle of which was the Townhall, with a clock-tower and a weather-cock. There were houses of stone, houses of red brick, houses of yellow brick, houses of plaster, and houses of wood, many of them very old, with withered faces carved upon the beams and staring down into the street. These had very little, winking windows and low-arched doors, and, in some of the narrow ways, quite overhung the pavement. The streets were very clean, very sunny, very empty, and very dull. Nothing seemed to be going on but the clocks and they had such drowsy faces; such heavy, lazy hands; and such cracked voices that they surely must have been too slow. The very dogs were asleep.

Rumbling along with most unwonted noise, the caravan stopped at last at the place of exhibition, where Nell dismounted amidst an admiring group of children, who evidently supposed her to be one of the wax figures. The chests were soon taken in to be unlocked by Mrs. Jarley, who, attended by George and another man, was waiting to decorate the room with the red festoons and other ornaments that came from the chests.

As the stupendous collection was yet concealed by cloths, lest the dust should injure their complexions, Nell bestirred herself to help and her grandfather also was of great service. The two men being well used to it, did a great deal in a short time; and Mrs. Jarley served out the tin tacks from a linen pocket which she wore for the purpose.

When the festoons were all put up as tastily as they might be, the stupendous collection was uncovered. There were displayed, on a raised platform some two feet from the floor, running round the room and parted from the public by a crimson rope, a number of wax figures as big as life, singly and in groups. They were clad in glittering dresses of various climes and times, and standing more or less unsteadily upon their legs, with their eyes wide open, and all their faces expressing great surprise. All the gentlemen were very pigeon-breasted and very blue about the beards, and all the ladies and all the gentlemen were looking intensely nowhere, and staring with extraordinary earnestness at nothing.

When Nell was over her first joy at this glorious sight, Mrs. Jarley gave her a willow wand, long used by herself for pointing out the characters, and was at great pains to tell her just what she must do.

Soon Nell knew all about the fat man, and the thin man, the tall man, the short man, the wild boy of the woods, and other historical characters. And so apt was she to remember them all, that she was soon perfectly able to guide all visitors.

222

THROUGH FAIRY HALLS

Mrs. Jarley then took her young friend and pupil to see the other arrangements. The passage had been changed into a grove of green cloth, hung with the inscriptions she had already seen. A highly ornamented table was placed at the upper end for Mrs. Jarley herself, where she was to sit and take the money, in company with his Majesty King George the Third, Mary Queen of Scots, and other important personages. The preparations without doors had not been neglected either for a beautiful nun was standing on a balcony over the door, and a brigand with the blackest possible head of hair and the clearest possible complexion, was being taken round the town in a cart.

In the midst of the various plans for attracting visitors to the show, little Nell was not forgotten. Decorated with paper flowers, she was given a seat beside the Brigand in the cart dressed with flags and streamers, wherein he rode. In this state and ceremony, she rode slowly through the town every morning, giving out handbills from a basket, to the sound of drum and trumpet. The beauty of the child, coupled with her gentle bearing, produced quite a sensation in the little country place. Grown-up folks began to be interested in the bright-eyed girl, and some score of little boys left nuts and apples, directed to her, at the wax-work door. All this interest in Nell was not lost upon Mrs. Jarley, who soon sent the Brigand out alone again, and kept Nell in the show-room, so that the people who were interested in her, would pay to come inside, where she described the figures every half-hour to the great satisfaction of all.

Although her duties were not easy, Nell found in the lady of the caravan a very kind and considerate person, who not only liked to be comfortable herself, but wished to make everybody about her comfortable also. So Nell and her grandfather found a comfortable home for some time with

MRS. JARLEY'S WAX-WORK

THE FOUNTAIN*
JAMES RUSSELL LOWELL

INTO the sunshine,
  Full of the light,
Leaping and flashing
  From morn till night;

  Into the moonlight,
    Whiter than snow,
  Waving so flower-like
    When the winds blow;

    Into the starlight
      Rushing in spray,
    Happy at midnight,
      Happy by day.

*In the fine tone poem, *The Fountain*, the French composer, Maurice Ravel, makes the listener see just what this poem describes—a fountain rising in the air, glittering in the sunshine, then splashing back into the pool.